CHASING CINDERELLA

Broken Dreams

By A.C.K. Min

Chasing Cinderella : Broken Dreams by A.C.K. Min
Published by Isabella Media Inc 270 Bellevue Ave #1002,
Newport RI 02840
www.IsabellaMedia.com

ISBN-10: 0-9994459-9-5
ISBN-13: 978-0-9994459-9-0

For permissions contact: requests@isabellamedia.com

CONTENTS

Acknowledgements

The author would like to express his gratitude and appreciation to the following people and organisation who contributed greatly to this book project:

(In no order of merit)

Crystal Learning Centre (Sponsor)

Edmund Ang

Giselle Qi

Janice Quah

Wilson Lee

Cover page design by Aurélie Charmeau.

Ngurunguur's Re-Dreamings

After an hour spent on a tree branch, the blue-winged kookaburra finally made its move. It swopped down swiftly on a baby mouse on the forest floor and ended the life of the tiny, brown rodent with its claws. The hapless mouse managed to let out only a stifled half shriek that was barely audible. Yet, its death was not without significance. Besides being a source of temporary nourishment to the bird, its passing meant the termination of the sufferings of a band of warriors from eons ago. Their stories could finally be laid to rest millennia after their bodies have rot away and became fodder for the storyteller's imagination.

It was a story that has been repeated for generations. Ngurunguur, the first storyteller ever, had forgotten how many times he had retold it. When he walked the scorched earth of the deserts in his land, he never saw the need to change the plot. Like the desert that was constant in its harshness, every retelling by Ngurunguur was unaltered. And so the successive generations of storytellers of his people kept the tradition and faithfully repeated Ngurunguur's story without any alteration.

Like many other nights under the sparkling diamonds that dot the desert sky, Ngurunguur's people sat around the fire after their nightly meal. They eagerly awaited one of Ngurunguur's many stories to incite their imagination and prepare themselves for their own dreams when they sleep. Dreams are stories imparted to them by their forefathers, they believed. A night's sleep without dreams meant that their past have abandoned them as their ancestors refused to communicate with them and that their night's rest would be incomplete. And so now, like other nights in the desert habitat, the expert storyteller begins:

"Out of the dark, milky solution, the black python stirred. Its first movement – lateral, tiny shakes of its muscle fibres which have been dormant ever since it created the cosmic milk that the reptile needed to sustain itself, caused innumerable undissolved flakes to dislodge from the vast expanse of the python's dark world into the sky-world that was nearer to the realm of men and Earth. The stars were thus formed. For the python's dark, viscous realm of existence was far beyond that of men and Earth and could only be reached after travelling to the farthest end of the sky-world. But one day, a tribe of the bravest but also the most desperate men of the land of men and Earth ventured out to look for food. Their wives, children and parents have been starving. They lived on an island and have never been in contact with anyone else. Fishing and gathering of fruits were what sustained them. Then came the terrible season. The sea around the island turned yellow and fish, which were once plentiful, were nowhere to be found. After two weeks (having eaten all the fruits – bananas, coconuts and mangoes, on the isolated island), there was nothing left. The only way was to row their boats out to search for other lands – something that had never been achieved. The island tribe had a fable about a young girl who rowed out to the sea and never returned. One day, the girl found a strange, foreign object on the beach of purple sand. She picked it up and saw the picture of a man's face. She knew that the man did not belong to the island for this man had red, curly hair and a yellowish face. Her people had black hair that was long and straight and their skin was of a dark chocolate colour. As if possessed and a spell was cast on her, the young girl stole a boat and rowed out to the vast ocean, never to return. Every islander knew this tale from birth. None dared to venture out except for the fishermen who made sure they tied their boats with ropes to other boats and at least one boat – usually the one nearest to the shore, had a rope secured to a pole on land. Their style of spear fishing did not require them to row out into the deep sea anyway. Still, the tale of the missing young girl spooked even the bravest fishermen among them.

The islanders were left with no choice in that terrible season. So, the strongest, bravest young men were gathered to save the tribe

 CHASING CINDERELLA — BROKEN DREAMS BY A.C.K. MIN

from dying of starvation. They will row out to find food – fish, sea birds or another lands, and return to save their families. They gathered their boats – there were five boats and twenty men in total, and bade a tearful farewell to their families on a bright, sunny morning. The sea was calm, though still slightly yellowish. Soon, they were nothing but a tiny speck on the horizon to the families that they had left behind on the shore. The desperate but brave men rowed for days without rest as they knew that their families depended on them. Despite their relentless effort, there were no fish, no sea birds and finally, no land as well. Sad, fearful and weak, they decided to tie their boats together with ropes. This way, only a few needed to row while the others took turns to rest. There came a point when there was no more day and there was only night. Using the stars as their guide, they simply rowed towards any star they saw. It did not matter which star they followed as they were too tired to care and the ones who took over the rowing were not instructed well by the ones who were rowing before. Stars were all they saw and they rowed towards them, all of them. In their fatigue and delirium, the young men did not even realise that they have fallen off the edge of the world of men and Earth and were traversing in the sky-world towards the python that stirred every now and then in its eternal slumber.

They must have rowed to their deaths. They had forgotten the last time they ate or saw their families back on the tropical island far, far away. By the time they saw the python slithering in its darkness – for by now the starlight from the sky-world were permanently lit in their eyes, the young men were skin and bones. Sallow, with bulging foreheads bigger than their pathetic tummies, the men looked like crazed demons. They jumped off their boats and seized the python. Drive by insane hunger, the island men sank their teeth into the python's flesh. Gnashing, biting, cutting, gnawing. They behaved like dingoes and not men. These demons from Earth must have their fill before they can get back home with the remainder of the python to feed their tribe. The python trashed about violently as the crazed island men bit off chunks of its flesh. If it could scream, its cries would have filled the realm with blood curdling shrieks. No matter how hard it tried, the men would not let it go. They sank their long, untrimmed fingernails into the python's body. Even as the python tried to coil its slithery self around the men to kill them, it was futile as there were too many of them attacking the snake from all sides. Some of the men even tied their long, unkempt beards to the reptile so that their jaws will never leave its succulent flesh. They kept chomping away, driven by blood lust. It was a crazy, frenzied scene. The only thing the python could do was to move across the space-realm – staying put at any one spot without moving was too painful. By then, the island men had forgotten why they were there in the first place and what their mission was. Eating became their obsession after the eternity that they have endured from rowing through such vast spaces. The python – with the men still suckling it like it was their blood mother, would reach the world of men and Earth. It writhed about in the sky, dripping blood that would form the burning magma in volcano craters. Its tears would create rivers, streams and waterfalls. When its tortured, exhausted and ravaged body fell from the sky and onto land, a long, winding and ragged path in the desert was etched. As the men who had forsaken their starving families fell from the sky and onto the ground below, they became rocks. Future people would use them to build houses in the deserts as punishment for their selfishness. They would forever bake under the hot sun and witness the warmth of family but never to feel such love again. Every year, the sky will turn red for a few days to remind people not to forget the python and the men's wretched selfishness. It was through the python's sacrifice that rivers, streams and lava enriched the earth. The desert path would lead to the ocean from inland, providing tribes with the chance to use the ocean's catch and bring food home for their families."

It was in this way that the story of the warriors and their treachery was told and retold for 50,000 years. There were no compelling reasons to change it. The desert, its landscape and the basic desires of the people who lived there, did not change. In the story, Ngurunguur's descendants understood the reasons, explanations and a narrative that justified everything in their worldly existence. So, they were careful of the wickedness of nature's seasons, climatic changes and the selfish wants of people. It taught them how to survive and appreciate all that they were given in the harsh environment. Evil deeds will be punished and the desert inhabitants learnt to look after one another.

The tale of the python and the deranged warriors told by Ngurunguur maintained the social fabric of his tribe. Though his story attained immortality (provided his people never become extinct), Ngurunguur himself was a mere mortal like any other who had walked the face of the Earth. He never really committed any sin in the same vein as that of the warriors in his story. In his lifetime, he was an obedient son, a faithful friend, a loyal husband and a responsible father. Yet, as a storyteller, he was guilty of a great misdemeanour – that of a total lack of originality. His greatest feat – to have a story unvarnished and unaltered from its inception for 50,000 years, was also his greatest failing. The fact that he did come up with the story in the first place did not matter that much. It was his duty as a storyteller to have stories in the first place. The lack of reinvention condemned him to an afterlife of retelling the one story that etched his name in folklore.

Death turned out to be a lot harder than living. While there is an ending to life, there is no end to death. Death is the constant in both states. In living, the constant is death as everything living must die at some point. In death, staying dead for all eternity is the constant. (Reincarnation is not a given. It depends largely on the belief system of the person. Even if the person's belief allows for reincarnation, some do not get the chance to reincarnate at all). The fate of dead storytellers is no different from that of any other professions. However, they have a distinct challenge. They have to continue to amuse in the afterlife (like they had done while alive) everyone else who's dead. This is the toughest job for any soul in hell. While alive, unless one's job requires one to tell stories, one can get by with knowing very few stories – real or fictional. It is not the duty of a janitor, a taxi driver, a lawyer, an athlete, an architect (and the list goes on) to spin a yarn. Hence, in the mortal world, storytellers do not have such a difficult time compared to the eternity they will spend in the afterlife. Not everyone knows every single story that was ever told. But it is different in hell. With time suspended, there is nothing much else to do in hell except to listen to stories. Even the sinners being tortured cannot escape from the incessant, booming voices of Homer, of Vyasa, of Luo, of Andersen, of

Dante, of the Grimm's, of Shakespeare, of the Bronte's, of Dickens, of Hemingway *et al*, who occupy every conceivable space in that infinite and interminable realm of endlessness. Even as Sisyphus pushed that god damn rock up the cursed mountain for the ten trillionth time (who's counting, anyway?), he could not avoid being bombarded by stories of monkey gods retold to him by some Indian or Chinese storyteller yakking away. Sometimes, the storytellers even accompany him by his side while he trudged up the mountain. Sisyphus cannot decide if his ancient, eternal punishment was worse than having to listen to the never ending drivel of the omnipresent blabbermouths.

Together with a hell lot of others, Sisyphus' plight is shared by the Devil himself. Presider and Owner of the Afterlife, of Hades, of Hell, of Eternal Punishments, the Devil's entire existence has been one that is inundated by all sorts of tall tales. From origins lore to satire fiction that mocked the existence of a creator to those that tried to counter atheist paradigm only to reaffirm the irrefutability of the devil, the Devil himself has heard it all. It has been a tiring and frustrating existence. And mortals wonder where the Devil got his tricks from. It was from them mortal storytellers spinning tales of blood sucking demons that morphed from one form to another that the Devil derived the inspiration to haunt and harass the living. He was merely doing what people's imagination had conjured up, thanks to the creativity of the storytellers. Without their input and innovation, the Devil will be nothing but a fallen angel and an agent of temptation in the form of a slithering reptile. Thanks to them, he could be whatever he wanted – a beautiful woman, a horny goat, a bat driven by blood lust, a vengeful dragon, a magician with queer glasses, or a hideous apparition… He has the storytellers to thank for striking fear in people's hearts. Yet, the Devil has mixed feelings about their continued and indefinite residency in his realm because of their eternal lack of originality.

Things have to change. Even the Devil can be spooked by the prospect of yet another endless epoch listening to the same material over and over. At once, using his supreme command over all beings in the realm under his charge, he summoned all the dead storytellers to appear before him. There must have been tens of thousands of storytellers gathered before the Devil to hear what he has to say to them. It was an unusual scene as no one has ever heard the Devil speak. Until now, words from him were not necessary in the underworld. He always had his underlings read out the sins committed by the dead while they were alive and to mete out their punishments to them. So, the storytellers thought to themselves, this announcement by the Devil himself must be one of ground-breaking importance.

"Each of you have an opportunity. Tell a new tale, a new story. You can use your existing plot but you must inject originality into it to make it fresh. I will be the sole judge as to whether your new version makes the cut. Bore me and I will expel your soul forever. Amuse me, delight me, entertain me with something new, and you will receive the gift of life again. I'm sure all of you are dying to get back to the mortal world, away from this insufferable place. In this world of the afterlife, I'm always present anywhere and everywhere. So, any of you can begin to tell your story anywhere and at any time. I'm always listening."

Hell became abuzz after the Devil's announcement. A chance to be released from hell's shackles and relive the pleasures they had once experienced in their mortal flesh? It is an opportunity not many would pass up on. Being in hell conferred upon the dead a kind of immortality. But it is a meaningless one. Immortality makes sense only when not everyone else has it. Also, it has value only when others around the immortals have their mortality under threat – in other words, in a place where everyone can exist indefinitely in a state of death, no one is ever in danger of dying since they are all already dead. Hence, there is not use in being "immortal" in hell. They did not forget that it is their punishment to exist forever in Hades. The Devil's offer is too tempting.

Being the oldest storyteller, Ngurunguur felt that he must take the lead in reinventing his stories. He had already gotten tired of telling and retelling stories – *any* stories and not just his old, rehashed ones. To recite amidst a crowd who did not care and even loathe his numerous recollections of past narratives – that was not how Ngurunguur wanted to spend the rest of forever. Death was now no longer the end point for him and the others. The Devil once again has succeeded in planting the seeds of temptation in souls. But what did he do except to offer a choice? Ultimately, the soul chooses. The Devil had never set any plot in stone for anyone. That is the main difference between him and those who craft storylines.

It was not just a matter of living up to his name that Ngurunguur felt obliged to be the first to attempt to win the prize offered by the Devil. He longed for a night under the sparkling stars. He missed those years when he was carefree and slept in the cool desert under the moonlight. When his people were all asleep and invoked dreams inspired by his night-time storytelling, he looked at the stars and wondered who lived there and how their lives were. He imagined himself visiting the stars. He would hop from one star to another, collecting the dreams of the people who lived there and then returning to his people and sharing his new stories with them. His people would then dream of strange lands and new people with new tales and plots. Over time, there would be enough ingenuity in their dreams for them to give to their children and their children's children a new, imagined world. But first, Ngurunguur has to bridge the distance between him and the stars.

Ngurunguur never shared all that went on in his mind while he was alone and excited under the sky at night. The young island girl in his story who saw the picture of the man with the red, curly hair dared to do what he merely contemplated in his mind. If he shared his wild thoughts of jumping from star to star with his people, it will also mean that he will cut across the vast space between them and the stars, much like how the girl dared to venture out into the endless ocean but never to return. Ngurunguur's star-hopping idea would scare his people too much. It would also remind them of the treacherous warriors who crossed the world of men into the sky-world and then into the python's dark, milky world. Did the act of crossing realms turn the men into degenerates? Was Ngurunguur himself thinking of transforming into a dangerous madman by dreaming of going to realms beyond? Ngurunguur knew his people too well. He simply cannot share his ideas with them because they would cast him out and he would never get to share his stories with them again. When he finally died in his sleep under the stars one night (his people found him half eaten by dingoes and his body was dragged deep into an uninhabitable part of the desert miles from the nearest human dwelling), his soul rose up and reached for the sky-world. But the Devil, with his tentacles reaching out everywhere on Earth where there are people dying, pulled Ngurunguur back down and into the deep recesses of hell beneath the ground where his tattered body lay.

In hell, there were no sparkling specks of light that Ngurunguur can look up to. Now, the Devil has offered him a chance to return to the mortal world and he could try, like the warriors in his story, to reach the sky-realm to save his arid soul from its long suppressed desire. Having been in this afterworld with no sunlight, moonlight and starlight for so long, the spark within Ngurunguur has all but flickered out. He could now only attempt to ignite the flame within so as to realise his desire to return to the mortal world. His jaded soul needed to forget all his oft-repeated tales and conjure up something novel to win the Devil's approbation. Ngurunguur sat down and closed his eyes. He imagined himself lying on the cool desert floor countless years ago looking up deep into the darkness hanging over him. And he began, he hoped, for the last time:

"Kuparr knew that it will not last much longer. Soon, he will no longer feel the scorching heat of the sun burning his insides. Lying face up, skin can be found only on his back — the rest had either been scraped, torn off by predators or had peeled off from the long, harsh exposure to the desert sun. What remained of him were parched and desiccated like the desert floor that they were stuck on. He had tried to get up before. But he quickly lay back down before he tore the skin on his entire back. The earth was cooking him alive. It had been slowly roasting what was left on his back for hours. The irony was that he did not need any cooking at all to become food. For hours, wild animals had been feasting on him. It started with his eyes. He remembered seeing the beak and two dark pupils staring at him before experiencing the penetrating pain in his eye socket; the strong, unyielding beak akin to an unrelenting spear poking, poking and poking…

Over and over, he could only guess where the pain came from. It was easy when there was only one thing eating him. Cold, hard teeth jabbing, tearing, gnawing, scraping his left rib, or his soft belly and further inside (that's where the delicious and nutritious parts resided), or his right thigh… A pack of animals crunching different bones in different parts of his body – that was sheer torture and it was made worse because of the unpredictability of the timing and location of the pain. Where was it coming from? Was there only one carnivore munching away at his left calf, or two, three, five? Should he be concerned that his neck will be next? The fatal bite to end all bites and his pathetic, lifeless existence never came. There was no need to bite his neck or crunch his skull since Kuparr has been inert all along. He did not fight back as he simply could not. His enemies knocked him unconscious and left him for dead in the desert. It was not long before the animals came for him.

Death would not come easily to Kuparr. Birds and animals have been picking and licking his bare flesh, snacking on some flesh and bone sticking out from his almost emptied chest and belly, crunching at his shin bone, playing with him like a treat to be wasted. With some life still left in him, Kuparr probably had a few more minutes of suffering left to endure. He wished that his suffering would end soon and that it never happened. He was sorry for seducing the chieftain's wife and then deflowering his twin daughters. But he cannot undo his sins. Now, he sought to quicken his end. Yet, all life in the desert seemed to be tired of his flesh and bones at this very moment. Only the heat from the sun and the bare earth were hastening his end. But it was an excruciating and interminable process. How long more?

Even as the desert's mid-day sun shone mercilessly on all forms of life everywhere, Kuparr's world was in complete, utter darkness. His eyes were now being digested in the guts of a few different birds and he did not know when his wretched last moments on Earth will be fleshed out. Pain was everywhere and he was still not dead. He thought of the nights that he spent alone, cast away from everyone because of his propensity to want to lay with every woman he saw. He was reckless and relentless in his pursuit of women. As soon as he entered manhood and the desires flooded him like any young man, there was no woman that was spared. His sisters, his female cousins; when he got older and stronger, even his older aunts and his mother became his conquests. He never asked for permission, of course. When he was just a younger teenager, he would just grope and rub himself on the younger women. Once he was a man, he violated every woman that he could get hold of. Eventually, the men in the village had to grab him and tie him up with ropes and dump him in a wooden cage. An animal like him belonged in captivity and should not be allowed to roam freely and endanger womenfolk as well as sully the honour of the men.

No one cared much for him. The village merely got an old woman to give him food and water once a day. Kuparr tried seducing, tricking and pleading with the old hen to regain his freedom. But she was deaf, mute and blind. She had long forgotten the pleasures that a woman can receive from a man. In any case, she no longer cared much about those feelings any more. The old woman just wanted to sleep as much as she could day and night. Feeding Kuparr was the only thing she needed to do in exchange for her carefree life. She was impervious to Kuparr's advances. Left with no other means of escape, Kuparr did what any rat like him would do. He gnawed for days using his bare teeth at the ropes that bound his wrists. The fibres in the ropes became a wretched form of sustenance for the caged pervert. It took him almost a fortnight to accomplish that feat. By then, his lips were chaffed and half of his teeth had fallen off from the effort. His gums were bleeding, too, and the corners of his mouth were cut open. It was nevertheless worth it. With his hands freed, he untied the ropes at his ankles and lay in wait for the moment when the old woman came to unlock his cage to feed him. Once she unlocked his tiny wooden prison, he pushed open the trap door as hard as he could and ran away like a savage freed from captivity. He ran for hours on end and no one in the village would hear from him or see him until half a year later.

Kuparr found freedom in the middle of the desert. Every night, he sat alone in the cold under the stars. He had nothing to do except to look at the scar marks on his wrists and ankles. If he had a mirror, he could look at his rotten mouth too. Away from civilisation, there was no one to judge him. Yet, nothing he could have done there mattered to anyone. But there was no one to defile, no soul to tempt, no honour codes to breach and no social conventions to transgress. He had all the liberty to do anything he wanted. True freedom was within his grasp. It was just that he had nothing to do and no one to do it to or with. Kuparr was in an unbounded prison.

He knew that he could never go back to his village. Death would be the outcome. They had been merciful to him despite what he had done. Now that he has escaped, they would not hesitate to kill him and rid the world of a scum like him. The villagers have been living in fear ever since Kuparr escaped, not knowing if he might return and wreak havoc to their lives, again. They should have eliminated that threat when they had the chance. Now, they just have to live in fear and regret. Kuparr lay his tired and malnourished body down on the desert floor. He was exhausted from thinking of his options. No matter how hard he tried, he cannot find a way out except to return to the village and beg for food, for shelter, for forgiveness, for an end to his plight. That night as he lay down and looked to the sky for answers, he saw the full moon. Why was the moon always so bright, Kuparr thought. The only explanation must be that there were lots of people lighting fires there. Unlike the coldness of the desert at night which he was experiencing at that very moment, he could be warm on the moon. If only he could escape from the desert and go to the moon and start afresh. No one there would know who he was and what he had done. He will not be known as a sinner and be an outcast. Life would start anew for him. Once again, he could do anything he desired. And that thought excited him. He was eager to see what sort of womenfolk were on the moon and how they might look like. Would they have arms and legs that are longer than what he has seen so far? Would their necks be shorter, longer, thicker? Would their skin be smooth like a rabbit's fur? Would the women cast him sly, sidelong glances or look at him boldly in his eyes and tell him what they want him to do to them? He was intrigued and thrilled to find out. It was then that the heavens presented Kuparr with an opportunity. No one else could have taken that chance like he could. Only a gifted degenerate with the most depraved perversion like him could have deciphered its meaning. Bit by bit, the full moon became smaller and smaller. The circle became less perfect and jagged edges appeared. It was as if another object, albeit a darker one, was covering up the brighter one. Since he was a child, he knew the story of the mating of the moon with the sun at night. Every child had that story told to them by their grandparents. The vigorous sun could not contain his exuberance and remain inactive at night. It wanted to be with the moon. But the moon was shy and did not want anyone to see them together behaving intimately. So, the moon whispered to the sun that she would only be with him if he came to her at night and covered himself such that he was completely dark like the night sky. But it took too much effort for the sun to shroud itself in complete darkness. Its nature and destiny was to always be the brightest object in the sky. Once it became dark, it felt the coldness of the night sky consuming him. It took him too long to recover from losing all his heat. Being with the moon could cost him his life. And so, the sun decided that he could only creep up on the moon once in a while. He needed to stay away from her and recover every time after they copulated.

Weak from hunger, Kuparr imagined that he was the sun. In his delirium, he fantasised that he was inching towards the moon. As his head got closer, the moon lost her brightness. She would gradually be consumed by the dark, bulbous blob that was his head which was filled with desires. Since his capture and captivity back in the village, he had no contact with anybody. Now, he would finally feel the warm femininity of the full moon. The coldness and the harshness of the desert would be forgotten, at least for a while, as Kuparr moved ever closer to achieve full contact with the bright moon for him to fornicate with it. The physical intimacy was like being with a woman – round and full; warm and embracing. His faults, his perversions, his depravity… all forgiven, all gone. She would take away his sins like a mother who would always forgive her child's mistakes no matter how severe they were. The moon would be his saviour. He could finally return to the village after and regain his former life. Yet, Kuparr was never one to be thankful and satisfied. He would simply relapse to his former atrocious behaviour back in the village and one day he would be cast back out again.

Kuparr knew that projecting his lascivious thoughts on the moon was not the way out of his predicament. He had his fun embracing, engulfing and blocking out the moon. But he needed more. More, so that he could have a new lease of life. Getting to the moon, to leave the desert, the village and the people who despised him – that was Kuparr's final goal. As he lay on the desert floor, he looked at the moon hanging high up in the sky looking down on him. She seemed to be mocking him, at his pathetic, exhausted body. 'Is that all that you have got? Covered me for a few seconds and then lay down tired and spent for the rest of eternity on the desert floor?' No, he thought to himself. He will do more than just penetrate her. He will own her. Kuparr willed himself to enter the moon, land on it, live there and own it. He would make her his, like those women back in the village. He would extinguish all the men and no one would oppose him and cast him out. With that in mind, Kuparr raised his right hand and tried to touch the moon. His right shoulder lifted slightly off the ground with the effort. Yes, he thought to himself, he could raise himself slowly into the night sky and get onto the moon. Moments earlier, he had just managed to embrace it, to make love to it. If he had managed to do that, getting onto the moon would just be a matter of effort.

Staring at the moon, Kuparr marshalled all the strength left in his body. He had to lift himself off the ground and float towards that bright, round object in the night sky. He was stuck on the desert floor and there was no way he could separate himself from it without tearing the remaining skin on his back. Nothing happened for a few minutes and he started breaking out in sweat in the cool, dry desert night. At first, there was a slight whimper, much like a dingo griping about being ignored by its pack. Then, it grew louder, more desperate, pleading, edgier and finally, angry – the dingo is now being eaten alive by its own kind. Kuparr screamed out in frustration that he cannot even lift himself half an inch off the ground. Defeated and utterly fatigued, he abandoned his quest and closed his eyes. Already weak from hunger and the cold, he cannot remember the sequence of events that led to his current state. Did he first escape from the wooden cage, found by the villagers and then finally beaten by them till he passed out and left for dead in the desert? Or did he never escape in the first place and was merely dragged by his haters out to the desert, clubbed unconscious and left there to die? He tried opening his eyes again to see the moon. He realised that he could not see anything. He had no eyes – they are already in the guts of some beasts somewhere. Kuparr cannot even have the moon in his eyes.

All the time, Kuparr was focused on what was above him. He thought that the moon would be his way out. He was mistaken. It was not what's up there that would decide his destiny. Underneath his inert body, deep in the bowels of Earth, a process had begun long before Kuparr was laid to waste there in the middle of no-where. Several million years ago, where Kuparr's village now lay, the sea flooded his home. It was submerged a few hundred metres be-low the sea. Instead of the dry, parched desert, it was an ocean that teemed with marine life. All sorts of prehistoric monsters and crea-tures lived in that ocean and relied on it for sustenance. From the voracious ichthyosaurs, to the formidable megalodon, to the placid sea turtle, to the omnipresent and harmless plankton, the sea habi-tat played host to a multitude of creatures over the course of its long history. Yet, the ocean had never seen a lifeform as bizarre and as re-sourceful as that of the winged sea cockroach. Like its land dwelling cousin, it can grow till as long as a grown man's little finger. Instead of using its wings to take flight, the sea cockroach uses its wings as fins to steer, propel and stabilise itself in the water. Although cockroaches have six legs, this marine bug only needed to use its two front legs and the two at its hind – the other pair in the middle were not really necessary for its movement. Hence, these two extra legs in the mid-section were shorter than the other four as they did not serve any practical function. The sea cockroach could choose to either scurry around on the ocean floor or take to swimming in the depths of the ocean. Alone, it was inconsequential and harm-less. Even a small fish could take the bug in its mouth and devour it. However, the might of the sea cockroach lay in the fact that it works with hundreds of thousands of others of its kind. Much like bees and ants on land, the sea cockroach moved about in swarms.

What made them a lot deadlier and fearsome was that they were purely carnivorous, unlike ants that may choose vegetation as part of its diet. Also, unlike bees that mostly defended themselves only when threatened, these sea bugs actively sought out prey. They can be likened to murderous and ravenous locusts of the sea that went after other animals. With a love for blood, these gangs of rapacious insects were constantly looking for their next kill. It does not matter if their prey was the size of a megalodon. In fact, the larger their kill, the more there was for every cockroach. There was nothing more terrifying than seeing an entire horde of them spiralling in a large, dark brown mass in the ocean and zooming in on their meal. The tornado-like vortex quickly swooped onto its prey, overwhelmed the poor animal by their sheer numbers and quickly entered any orifice – the gills, the eyes, the slightest opening of the mouth, to access the insides of the doomed creature. It was impossible to stop them. Once inside, they would coordinate like a well-trained army. Scores of them would focus just on one spot. They would bite, tear and chew at that spot with their mandibles and maxillae together at once. Alone, their feeble insect mouth parts would not inflict significant damage even to the insides of their victims. But together, working in gangs of dozens and then multiply that by several thousands of times at many different points inside their prey, it became a deadly strategy. The bursting of blood vessels would soon cause massive internal bleeding and cut off vital circulation to the rest of the animal's body. That was the essence of their work. The tearing of the marine creatures from the inside would cause flesh, tissue, cartilage, bodily fluids and everything else to spill into the waters that encapsulated them. It was the closest thing to implanting dynamites inside the victims' bodies and blowing them up. A feeding frenzy would ensue and once over, the deadly insects would move on to their next prey.

The sea cockroaches used that method to deadly effect for eons. Their brutality and speed made them the apex predator of the ocean. Yet, their very success meant that their sources of food were being depleted at an exponential rate. With increasing numbers of their kind due to their supremely efficient feeding tactic, it was impossible to sustain their collective appetite in the long term. The cockroaches started to compete against their own kind for the limited food sources that have grown increasingly sparse over time. Gangs of them – hundreds of thousands per group, would pit against each other. It was through such intense rivalry that these wonderfully wicked creatures found a way to forever end their hunt for food. It was possible to hunt only once and an everlasting food source would sustain them forever. This would relieve them of the tiresome burden of having to endlessly look for food. Once, a formidable gang tore up a sperm whale from the inside and threw up everything into the immediate region. This gang of irrepressible bugs proceeded to feed as usual. Not far away was another gang of sea cockroaches. Capitalising on this opportunity for an easy feed, this second gang swooped in onto the unsuspecting killers of the sperm whale. Overly engrossed, the first gang took no notice of the second gang. Forming a deadly vortex from below the first gang to avoid detection, the opportunists rose rapidly from the ocean floor and engulfed the victims and their food. A hurricane-like whirlpool of sea cockroaches caught the first gang by surprise. They were spun around inside this vortex together with the meat, bone and teeth of the sperm whale with rapid speed. The bone and teeth of the deceased whale acted like blades to shred into pieces everything in the deadly vortex. A few seconds of this would suffice to destroy the cockroaches in the first gang. Yet, the second gang did not relent for a few minutes. It went on and on, and in fact, it lasted for an hour. The incredible force that it generated started to churn the waters around it. Within the vortex, everything had been grinded and blended into a milky solution. Now, with the inexorable force created by it, things around the vortex were drawn into the kill zone, decimated and then they too – oceanic creatures of all types and sizes: coral, marine vegetation, rocks and basically anything and everything unfortunate enough to be in the vicinity, became part of the milky solution. It went on for an hour as the second gang of cockroaches realised that while they were generating the vortex, they could also feed on the solution at the same time. Not every cockroach needed to be in the centre of the vortex. The vortex, due to its sheer size, needed many layers in order for a large enough force to be generated. The cockroaches in the innermost layer were the closest to the milky solution that was their food source. These cockroaches will feed on the solution and then move outwards to allow the other cockroaches in the outer layers to move inwards and then towards the centre of the vortex to feed on the milk. After this first experience, this gang of cockroaches realised that they had discovered the perfect way to generate their own renewable food source. Their second attempt at generating the killer vortex deep in the ocean would also be their last.

This discovery started a process that would see Kuparr move closer to his destiny. He would also learn about his true fate and that he was misled and misguided all along. Hours after that murderous destruction of their own kind, the voracious second gang of cockroaches felt the need to hunt again. They were insatiable not only in their desire for food but also in their ambition to recreate their new predatory tactic. They could outdo countless generations of their kind that came before them and turn themselves into the most successful species ever. It was their quest for immortality. They did not bother to wait for another gang of cockroaches to start their feed. Instead, they went straight for the kill by swooping from below an unsuspecting humpback whale. The dark brown tornado of ravenous cockroaches spun the poor whale thousands of times and it was already dead from convulsion in a matter of seconds. The formidable gang spun harder and faster. They were indefatigable. As the flesh and bone of the whale tore up, the cockroaches gathered strength from feeding on it. But this time, food was not their primary motive. They became obsessed with creating an ever-increasing force. The whirlpool got larger and deadlier as the surrounding waters got sucked into the fatal cyclone. As more and more marine plant life and creatures were sucked into it, the cockroaches mustered more energy from having more to feed. It became a self-sustaining ecosystem on its own after an hour. The cockroaches could go on and on as long as the milky solution sustained their lives. There was no need to stop as even when the cockroaches mated, laid eggs and produced more baby cockroaches in between feeding, the sheer size of the vortex meant that it was relatively stable despite the mayhem that it was creating in the ocean. Once the momentum was generated, very little effort was needed from each cockroach to keep the whirlpool from spinning and churning. It was like a hive that sustained itself by creating death to anything that fell into it. Days went by and the maelstrom in the ocean continued to swirl violently and inexorably. Weeks passed and more cockroaches were added to the deadly spinning hive. A month later, it became a monster of a hurricane in the depths of the sea. Small islands – together with the vegetation, animal and human life on them, fell victim to this deadly force of nature generated by the bugs. Rocks, knolls, thousand-year-old trees and even man-made structures were crushed and shattered to create the milky solution that sustained the killer insects.

It was a sight to behold – provided that one does not get violently sucked into the terrible storm brewing in the ocean. In the immediate vicinity of the carnage, it was possible to escape only if one was a bird flying above the water surface. Everything that came into contact with water (besides the air above it) got sucked in and then destroyed to make the milk for the cockroaches. Yet, this process cannot be sustained. The sea bugs did not give anything back to nature in this cycle. In consuming everything that nature produced, the cockroaches attained eternal life. The destruction of all life around them sustained their immortality and negated the timeless cycle of life and death.

In their relentless pursuit of wanton destruction, the cockroaches became blind, literally, to where they were heading. They need not see or know where they were going, since they created a path for themselves by destroying anything and everything that lay in their way. Even the angulation of their deathly whirlpool did not matter anymore. Vertically, horizontally or sideways, they headed wherever they wanted. This was how they tunnelled their way into the continental shelf and violently burrowed their way into the bedrock directly under the desert floor which Kuparr was lying in despair. As they drilled their way upwards and burst out explosively from under Kuparr, his body shattered into smithereens and it was at this moment that Kuparr could finally see what he has been doing wrong all this time. The connection between himself and the moon was never a physical one. It was a pipedream to think he could have bridged the vast distance between himself and the moon by travelling there in his mortal flesh. Now, as he looked at the thousands of bits that used to form his pathetic, ravaged shell only a few milliseconds ago, he was finally enlightened. He could never have reached the moon whilst alive. His depraved and perverted self, driven by the constant need for stimulation of his base senses, was never worthy of the refined and calm bearing of the moon. Losing his life, albeit violently, was the best thing that ever happened to Kuparr. Freed from the constraints imposed by his mortality, he could now make his journey towards his extra-terrestrial destination…"

THE COYOTE'S TALE

The souls wandered around the underworld and all listened keenly to Ngurunguur's newly concocted tale. Among the dead storytellers, there was a mixture of wonder and quiet indignation. They were not fully convinced that Ngurunguur should pass the Devil's test simply because he conjured up something new. It seemed obvious to many that Ngurunguur merely pieced together a fantastic tale of a native and married it to the familiar lore of escaping to the moon found in many ancient cultures. Was it even captivating? Was it worthy of induction as a yarn to be spun by future generations of tale spinners for all time? Everyone wanted a trip back to the mortal world. Why should Ngurunguur be the one just because he was first to the task? The Devil could very well change his mind after listening to Ngurunguur's twisted, mindless plot and suspend his reward out of sheer disgust.

It was anyone's game. They had nothing to lose and a lifetime to fight for. Just as Ngurunguur spoke of Kuparr's epiphanic breakthrough, Twisted came forth to start his story before Ngurunguur could continue. Twisted figured out that the Devil did not state that the story had to be told continuously by a single person and it was not stipulated that the reward of renewed life would be bestowed only on one storyteller. And so Twisted began another story just as Ngurunguur briefly paused:

"All the animals in the grasslands and forests had their uses. The bison fed the tribes, made the warriors strong and provided the nutrients for the womenfolk to feed their babies. Their hides were made into skins for the elders to decorate themselves, enabled the tribes to make moccasins and clothes and also provided the material for making tepees. Their bones and horns were used to make weapons, decorative head dresses, tools and dishes. Even their dung were used as fuel. The humble rabbit provided some meat for snacking and also allowed the young children to practice their hunting skills. So were the deer in the forests and fishes in the streams and rivers. Even the bear that slept for months in winter. Not just a source of food and hide, the bear symbolised courage and strength. To face a bear and kill it – that required courage. And even though the wolf was both hated and feared, its ferociousness and tenacity inspired many warriors to exhibit these qualities to deter enemies and also to win battles. The coyote was a different story and animal altogether. No one would eat a coyote – its meat tasted like dirt and it was too bony. There was just not enough flesh on it to justify the effort to hunt it. It was seen to be a waste of energy and effort hunting a solitary animal that yielded so little meat that tasted foul anyway. It was cunning and without morals. The coyote runs from a fight and seeks to hide to save its skin. Fathers would never want their sons to grow up to have coyote-like traits. Rather be hated and feared like a wolf than be mocked and ridiculed like a coyote. A woman who marries a coyote-like man must be prepared for a husband who is irresponsible and will bring harm to the family. Yet, the coyote, like any other animal of the grasslands and the forests, desires to be of use. Why can't it be like the horse? People love horses for it can carry loads and bring them hunting or to battle. But the coyote's back was too narrow for such tasks. Besides, it was too cowardly and lazy to perform those tasks. It was not delicious, not admired, nor coveted as a prized hunt like a bear for its head and a cougar for its countenance to decorate the head of a chieftain. There was no need for a coyote and no use for it. As a breed, they should have been cast out of existence.

Once, a coyote entered a village after midnight and saw a young child naked by the fire. The little girl was placed there by her father who lost his wife, the girl's mother, from an illness a few hours ago. He told his eldest son to keep watch over the little girl who was left near the fire to keep her warm as her mother's bosom had already turned cold. The coyote looked at the baby girl's plump, round body and thought to itself: 'What a delicious meal she would make!' But the eldest son sat on a log near her and had a tomahawk with him. So, the coyote went into an empty tent and stole a colourful blanket and covered itself with it. The coyote lay down on the ground in the darkness a few metres from the eldest son and began to whimper like a young woman. Spotting a body wrapped in a bright red cloth in the darkness not too far away, the eldest son became curious and slightly aroused by the mysterious feminine-like figure that lay on the ground. He walked towards the coyote that was in disguise with anticipation. Just when he was next to it and was starting to kneel down to touch the mysterious, whimpering creature, the coyote violently shook the blanket off itself and onto the young man's face and scampered towards the baby girl by the fire. It grabbed the baby with its jaws and ran off into the darkness of the woods nearby. When it was safe and far from its pursuer, the coyote prepared to feast on the crying baby girl. Saliva dripping from its gnashed fangs, it let out a high-pitched howl and thrust its sinewy neck towards the defenceless baby girl on the ground. Just then, a blinding, yellow glow flashed into the coyote's eyes, searing it with pain. The animal fell forward and sprawled on all fours on the ground, unable to move. The yellow glow emanated from a forest spirit who now stood before the coyote, towering over the creature.

'Why do you have to eat a baby?' The forest spirit asked in an accusatory tone.

'I hate people and eating their babies will get rid of them. But after they die, they just keep coming back again and again. Their spirits never leave the land. The more I kill, the more they will return. So, I must kill, eat, kill more, eat more, kill even more and eat even more,' the coyote gnarled while its eyes were still smarting from the pain.

'What do you want?' The spirit asked.

Now, the coyote could squint a little and it could make out the silhouette of a six-foot tree that towered over it. The tree was dripping with viscous liquid from its leaves and branches.

'People don't need me; I am of no use to them. So, I assigned myself the task of killing them as they have made my life a meaningless one. I find purpose in killing those who disregard me. Yet, I can never finish this task and the spirits of the people just keep coming back! What a hateful bunch! What a cursed purpose! But I must have a purpose!' The coyote howled.

'What should I do?' The coyote implored.

'All who die may not need to return. Send them to the spirit land where they will stay forever!' The forest spirit replied.

By now, the forest spirit was no longer six-foot tall but had shrunk into a tiny, purple shrub that was no bigger than the coyote's head. Still, the coyote was terrified of the forest spirit as it thought that the spirit was wicked and had magical powers that will harm it.

The coyote then learnt from the forest spirit that human spirits can be shut off from re-entering the world of the living after death. Every time someone dies, the medicine men would gather in a grass house that faced east. The black and white eagle feather on top of the grass house would become heavy with blood, droop and then fall over. That is when the medicine men would start to sing to attract the spirit of the person who had just died to enter the grass house. From outside, the medicine men would be heard chanting.

'Oh-oh, oh-oh. Eh, eh. Woe-ho.' The men would go on again and again, over and over and a gush of wind from the east would start to blow and move towards the grass house. The spirit of the recently deceased tribe member would be carried along with the wind and enter the hut through the easterly opening. Once inside, the chanting would cause the spirit to reassume its former human form. Death was only temporary for the people in the tribes.

The coyote would change that. With the information given by the forest spirit, the coyote had a new calling. It would be on the lookout for the black and white eagle feather on grass huts. Once the black and white eagle feather gets bloodied and droopy, the coyote would watch the grass house keenly for the arrival of the medicine men. It would creep closer once the first chants are heard. When the loose grass and tree twigs get picked up by the wind, the coyote would silently close the flap to the entrance of the grass house. The spirit would be unable to enter and the wind would simply blow past the grass house. Death became permanent to the spirit that cannot enter.

From then on, the coyote became an even more despised creature. Families wept and wailed, knowing that their dead will never return to them but will instead wander aimlessly in the forests and over the streams until they enter the underworld. And because they were expected to return to them, bereaved families did not prepare the items and tools that the dead will need in the afterlife. Hunting implements like bows and arrows, spears, daggers, and essential items like blankets and moccasins, for example, were not buried with the dead. The dead were condemned to an afterlife of starvation and coldness for eternity. The coyote was cursed and hunted down. Warrior bands were formed throughout the land. Armed to their teeth with weapons, they set fire to every burrow, smoked out every cave and poisoned every creek they could find to kill all and any coyote they could lay their hands on. But their ceaseless efforts for vengeance hurt the other animals and trees. The deer cried out when its young died from drinking the poisoned creek water. The bear moaned as it slept out in the cold during winter, having been evicted from its warm cave. Rabbits and wolverines could no longer hide in their once safe burrows. The land cried out in pain and wished for the hunt for the coyote to stop.

The forest spirit was devastated. It had wanted to help the coyote by giving it a purpose. Yet, by doing so, it caused great anguish to the land, the animals and the people. To make up for its guilt, the forest spirit decided to adopt a human form and to stop the destructive hunt for the coyote. It turned itself into an old, frail man who walked around with a thick, crooked tree branch. One evening, he wandered into a village just after sunset when the braves had just returned from one of their coyote hunts. He sat down near the fire where the village elders would discuss the day's happenings. The old man introduced himself to them as a wanderer who had been moving from land to land all his life and lived off from what nature had to offer him. He told them a fantastic tale that one day, while he was sleeping at night in a forest on a tree branch high above the ground like a jaguar, he heard some strange noises. He crept quietly along the tree branch to have a better look at what was going on. What he saw shocked and terrified him. But he managed to stifle a scream from his throat as he knew that if he let out any sound, his life would be in immediate danger. There was a burning, red glow coming from the forest floor. The amber glow from it illuminated the forest in the darkness of the night and the old man, despite his failing vision, could see a coyote crouching on the floor, fixated on something right in front of it. The glow came from a creature that was on fire. It was no ordinary creature. It was a demon. It had to be. Nothing could ever be in flames and yet instruct another living thing with authority. The old man could not make out its exact shape. It was as if someone, or something, was completely engulfed in flames and its actual form cannot be ascertained. The old man strained his ears to hear what the flaming demon said to the coyote.

'Inch by inch, I crept closer to them and I was very careful not to lose my balance and fall onto the forest floor. That will surely be the end of me! The demon told the coyote that humans must be punished for taking from the land for so long. Killing deer, hunting bisons and setting fire to clear forest land… I wondered to myself: 'What were we supposed to do? Die? That's survival!' Anyway, I listened quietly and heard the demon impart to the coyote a plan to stop people from coming back to life after they died. If the coyote followed the demon's orders, the dead will never return and this will be the punishment for humans who had also disrespected the coyote for so long. Hearing that, the coyote howled for minutes and leapt in the air. I have never seen a coyote leap so high before in my entire life!'

The old man was extremely animated when he recounted his experience in the forest. He hugged himself tightly and shook vi-olently to show that he was in fear while in the forest and leapt up to mimic the coyote's jump. He also tried to sound like the coyote when it was howling in the forest. The village elders and everyone else who had gathered to hear the stranger's tale were impressed by the old man's energy. He looked like a young brave filled with enthusiastic passion and not a geriatric who needed a walking stick. From his tale, the villagers realised that the coyote was not totally at fault. It was the demon who instigated the plot to stop the dead from coming back to life. The hunt for the coyote was a meaningless one. If they wanted to solve the problem, they must somehow find the demon and get rid of it. Word spread quickly through the land and the hunters and the braves stopped their bloody hunt for the coyote. Instead, shaman bands started to form. The shamans of the different tribes got together to find out what was the nature of this mysterious demon that had the evil and cruel plan to part the living from the dead forever. They had never heard of such a spirit or form from their forefathers. Even the oldest and the wisest shaman of the land was puzzled.

The old man went from village to village, from tribe to tribe, to spread his tale. He wanted everyone to get his message so that the hunt for the coyote will stop. In essence, though, the old man was still a forest spirit and he needed to be near a forest every few weeks to sustain his life force. Otherwise, he would not be able to maintain his human form and would revert to his original form of the forest spirit. However, in his zeal, he wandered farther and farther away from the forested areas and ended up in the freezing north where he stumbled upon the Inuits. It was upon arriving there that he realised his foolishness – the coyote did not live so far up north. The old man turned back immediately and quickened his pace, for he needed to be reunited with the energy of the forest as soon as he could. It was almost a month and a half of walking in the southerly direction before he neared a forest clearing. By then, he was completely exhausted and he collapsed just before the clearing. A band of hunters returning from an expedition saw him and carried his frail, almost lifeless body back to their village. Unfortunately for the forest spirit, the village was located deep in a valley devoid of any trees. By saving him, the hunters took him farther from the forest which sustained him. The village elders recognised him as the storyteller who excitedly told them of the demon who was the mastermind behind the coyote's treacherous deed. The elders housed him in a hut and tried to save his lifeless body for several days.

Yet, as each day went by, the old man increasingly looked more pale and kept getting thinner and thinner. Finally, at the end of a month, the old man turned into a twig. A young girl ran out of the hut shouting hysterically one afternoon after she was instructed to bring some water to the tent and look after the old man. The village elders rushed into the tent, only to see a twig instead of the old man lying on the bear skin laid out on the ground. They called in the medicine man who was also the shaman. Sitting crossed legged on the ground, the shaman went into a trance after boiling some peyote in water. He sat very still for an hour and then sprinkled some crushed salvia leaves that he had brought with him in a small basket woven from the fibres of sea grass. No one left or entered the tent for the next three days. At the end of the third day, the shaman stepped out of the tent and walked unsteadily to the village chief and brought him into the tent. They did not leave the tent for half a day and the villagers started to crowd around the tent excitedly. When the village chief finally stepped out, the sun had set and he asked for Screaming Horse, the most fearsome warrior in the village and told him to take his tomahawk with him into the tent. Seconds after Screaming Horse entered the tent, the villagers could hear a loud, dull thud. Soon after that, the chief, the shaman and Screaming Horse came out of the tent. Screaming Horse was holding something circular wrapped in a blood-stained cloth and everyone gasped when they saw it. Screaming Horse walked towards the nearest fire and tossed the object, together with the cloth it was wrapped in, unceremoniously into the flames. No one spoke a word that night. Screaming Horse returned to his tepee alone and slept. The chief and the shaman took the village elders into the chieftain's tent and all of them spent the night in it.

The next morning, the first person in the village who woke up saw a strange phenomenon in the valley. A young boy stepped out of his tepee and saw fresh, pale green shoots sprouting from the ground at the edge of the valley. In a matter of seconds, the shoots turned into tiny little weeds of a darker shade of green. And the weeds multiplied rapidly. Soon, in less than an hour, the entire valley was creeping with the weeds, which by now had adopted a bright, purplish hue. The weeds advanced into the village that was in the middle of the valley. The villagers did not have time to wake up when the weeds stormed towards the village with an alarming speed. The young boy, amused and curious at first, ran to the perimeter of the village to have a closer look. He was immediately covered with twines and weeds from head to toe and crushed by their relentless surge of desire to consume all that stood in their path. The weeds did not care for tall poles or tepees or livestock – all were subsumed under their cruel zeal to swallow up and squash anything and everything in that valley. No one had a chance to escape, except for Screaming Horse. He woke up just in time to see the tepee next to him being attacked by the creepers and vines. He reached for his tomahawk with the quickness he was famous for and ran out, hacking and slashing at anything that tried to touch him. Despite his strength and athleticism, the brave warrior was caught by vines that gripped his left arm and threatened to draw him back into the deathly zone of a sea of hungry, crawling vegetation. Screaming Horse desperately hacked away at his left arm just above his elbow. He was a brave warrior, but death in such a bizarre, meaningless fashion was just too much for him to accept. Screaming Horse must have had hacked at himself at least three times before the killer weeds finished the separation for him as the vines continuously pulled in towards the village. Once he was free, Screaming Horse ran for his life away from the village and the valley by climbing to higher ground above the sunken valley of death. His home was now covered in a mess of purple that had turned into a massive burial ground for his family, friends and tribe. Looking down at the valley with defiance, Screaming Horse licked the blood off his tomahawk with his tongue and swung his right arm far backwards, lunged his entire body forward and threw his tomahawk back down into the valley. He swore aloud that he would return to take revenge.

For days, Screaming Horse trotted on the plains on top of the small hill that overlooked the valley. It was the height of summer and the ground was parched. The grass had turned yellow from the dryness of not having rainfall for weeks. There was no animal in sight. Not even the coyote could be seen. Screaming Horse was weak from thirst and hunger. He could not see signs of any settlement nearby. Still, he knew he must stay alive to take his revenge. He found a withered tree and he sat straddled on one of its massive roots that protruded from the ground and leaned against the trunk. All he could do was to stare afar with dwindling hope that he would still be alive the next day. He was weak and hated himself for feeling that way. The warrior in him wanted to fight his fate and the treacherous weeds that destroyed his people. Yet, he knew that his ability to overcome his desperate situation was severely limited. Alone, without sight of help, how was he ever going to amass enough strength, let alone a band of braves, to exact revenge? But for now, he needed to rest. His eyelids felt heavy and he soon fell into a restful slumber.

He woke up two hours later. It was still light. The sun would not be setting for another three hours at least. Screaming Horse observed that there was something different with the view in front of him. Before he dozed off, the ground that extended before him was an endless stretch of yellow irregularly interspersed with some weak greenish hues. Now, he saw that the green patches were no more. Instead, there seemed to be blotches of black in the canvas before his eyes. At first, he thought the blazing sun had caused him to have a headache when he slept as he saw black dots moving about hurriedly before his eyes. Screaming Horse stood up slowly and took a few steps forward to better assess what he was seeing. The black patches moved closer and closer to him, he noticed. No longer were they tiny specks that zapped about with no discernible pattern. As the dots became larger, they were also moving about with greater speed and purpose. They were converging to a point. It did not take long for Screaming Horse to realise that they were coming towards him. He ran away from the tree and was relieved that they did not come after him. Instead, all the black patches converged onto the tree and in seconds, the withered tree – its roots, branches and trunk, were covered in a mass of black. The black death of dark-coloured termites had engulfed Screaming Horse's resting place. The tree was consumed by the devil's ants gracefully without sound or drama like it was a routine that they had rehearsed for countless times. Once the feasting was over, the black mass of ants on the naked tree branches fell gently back onto the ground where the other termites were. The collective of ants intuitively made room for their comrades that fell from height without any fuss. These were no ordinary termites for they eat not just wood, but any vegetation and maybe even more. With the tree gone, Screaming Horse was the only other living thing besides the ants themselves. Now that he was quite close to them, he could see clearly that each black ant was the size of his palm. They were voracious and ruthless. And as a group, their appetite is insatiable. The locust of ants now moved together and surged towards Screaming Horse who had already began to flee for his life.

Screaming Horse felt that he needed to grow a pair of wings and fly away to save himself. Running away from the termites was impossible. He moved his legs as fast as he could but whenever he turned his head to look behind every now and then, he saw that he did not increase the distance between him and the tiny monsters. Instead, they appeared to gain just a little bit on him every time he checked. He ran back to the valley as the path back into it was a narrow, winding one down the small hill. Screaming Horse hoped that the circuitous route would slow down his pursuers. It worked at first when Screaming Horse made sharp turns down the first few bends. However, to his horror, the termites became wiser and started to stream down the sides of the hill and bypassed the winding road. Screaming Horse stopped running as he saw that the termite swarm had gotten in front of him and also cut off his retreat with their new strategy. He knew that he was going to die. How he would die would be another matter. He could either stay where he was and be swallowed by the termite swarm like the withered tree before him, or he could die a warrior's death. Screaming Horse charged forward with his eyes closed. He was not far from the foot of the hill with just another few hundred yards to go down the winding path. With all his might, he ran forward and leapt high in the air. While he was jumping, he thought of the time when the village chief sent him on his solo journey into the wilderness to earn his right to be a warrior of the tribe. In the few days out in the wild, Screaming Horse connected with his spirit animal – the horse, that gave him the determination and the courage to survive on his own and trek back to his village. At night, to scare off the wolves, the young brave would let out a blood curdling cry that would become his trademark before he went to war against rival tribes. He became known throughout the region for his single-minded focus on victory in battle, along with his high-pitched yell. As he made that leap on that narrow path blocked by the murderous insects, he screamed himself hoarse as he knew that that would be the last time he would get to express himself. He landed and crushed the termite swarm with his four hooves. The warrior had now turned into his spirit animal and galloped without care down the path. Even as the vermins were stomped upon while giving chase, they never relented. Crawling down the sides of the hill, they managed to get onto the horse's body in increasing numbers. As he neared the foot of the hill, he was already half covered by termites. Still, he did not give up and continued to head towards his village that was by now a wasteland of purple weeds and vines. Just a bit more, the horse thought to himself, legs sprinting tirelessly to their final destination. He was exhausted from the sheer speed and the growing weight of the multitude of ants on him. At the edge of the wasteland, Screaming Horse could no longer sustain the weight and crashed onto his side. His horse-form body slid under the towering vines and was swallowed into the dense of weeds.

Screaming Horse exacted his revenge and he paid for it with his life. The sea of termites was now lured to the village of weeds and vines and started to devour the vegetation. The termites were in for a shock, though, as its meal was alive and vengeful. For every morsel that the termites took into their tiny bodies, death became nearer. The ever voracious vegetation continued with their destruction even after they were ingested by the insects. The weeds and vines multiplied inside the termites and caused every one of them to die when the new shoots burst from within the ants. In this way, the menace of the insect horde ended. Yet it marked the start of the recombination of Screaming Horse's soul. Having been previously devoured by thousands of termites that just had their physical bodies cast into the wind and soil, his soul was similarly dispersed and was everywhere and nowhere…"

THE BOY FROM NOWHERE

Ngurunguur had to do something. He cannot sit there and simply let Twisted take charge with his crazy tale that may upend his earlier effort. He started first. So why should he let someone else get in before he finished telling his story and overtake his efforts to win the Devil's reward? While alive, Twisted had condemned himself to a lifetime in hell because he did something gravely unforgiveable like the warriors who lost their original purpose in Ngurunguur's *Re-Dreamings*. His life on Earth was prematurely shortened because he invented the story of the coyote that stopped the dead from returning to life. From then on, Twisted's people died and never returned to life unlike before. His story terminated the endless cycle of life among the people of his land. Enraged, his people became berserk, skinned him alive and threw him into a cauldron of boiling water. Ngurunguur looked down on Twisted as no better than the depraved warriors in his tale for forsaking his own kind and he could not bear the thought of losing the prize to an inferior storyteller. As soon as Ngurunguur caught a break in Twisted's storytelling, he interrupted Twisted's unfinished tale of Screaming Horse's soul:

"As Kuparr looked at the thousands of parts that used to form his whole, infinite possibilities presented themselves. Each part of him was a life beyond himself. He wasn't always the village pervert who preyed on everyone. Like any, his life started out on a blank slate. As babies, the potential for good and evil was the same for everyone. He had a normal childhood like everyone else. His parents were decent, hardworking villagers who looked after the land and grew crops like the others in the village. His father was not a warrior like most men as he was frail and often sickly. Farming became a natural vocation for him since he was not included in the scouting and hunting bands. There was not a lot of fertile land in the arid environment and his father and mother often had to venture into the forest to pick wild vegetation and fruits for the village. Often, Kuparr was left by himself at home in their family hut made of mud and straw. Alone, the child had nothing to entertain himself with. Lying on the ground, with his view of the sky blocked by the mud roof of his family's hut, he conjured up images in his mind and made them talk and interact with one another. He never once verbalised his imaginations, preferring instead to think of plots, storylines and dialogues in his head. His parents never knew what went on in young Kuparr's mind as he often appeared to be merely staring into space or closing his eyes as if he was having a nap while he raised his characters from the vast spaces within his mind.

Now, with his death, Kuparr can once again invent new stories and characters out of thin air. In that instant when he realised he was dead and looked at his disparate body parts, he focused on a piece of flesh that flew away from the ground (like many others). There was no particular reason why Kuparr chose this one piece of flesh since it was no different from the others in colour and size and had no distinguishing characteristic. It could have been the stub of one of his fingers, a piece of his cheek, a small part of his thigh, a slice of his belly… It was just there and Kuparr happened to choose this specific one. From that tiny, insignificant piece of flesh, a new story begins:

‘A soirée was held to mark the coming of age of young men and women of the nobility. The Prince had not wanted to attend the function. At 18, he was awkward and shy. He did not like crowds and preferred to spend his time in the castle tower researching on magic spells and reading up the exploits of men on the battlefield who existed before his time. There were rumours whispered not so secretly in the beer halls and in the marketplace among petty thieves, gossipy women and ordinary folk that the Prince had learnt the dark art of transforming his personage by studying an ancient book from the land of Gommorah. The tome was said to be found among the war spoils of the army of Alexander of Macedonia buried in a sand pit outside the Oracle of Delphi hundreds of years ago. No one could be sure how it ended up in Keltulop. One version had it that an immortal shaman from the time of the prehistoric Xia Dynasty of China who vowed to circumnavigate the globe on foot dug up the treasures of Alexander's army in the hope of locating the special ability to walk on water mastered by Jesus and Bodhidarma. Hearing that the buried war booty contained the secrets of the Hindu sages who also learnt the story of parting water bodies from ancient Judea, the shaman brought the ancient book together with some other books of spells to Keltulop. He had hoped to get the books translated as he heard that Keltulop was famous for housing the five masters of the languages of the world. So happy was he to finally arrive in Keltulop after walking for three years without stopping that he forgot to honour his vow of meditating an entire night until first light whilst balancing his entire being on his forehead with his shaman staff placed horizontally on both feet every time he arrives in a new city that he spent the whole night entertaining the castle folk with his tales. When the sun's rays pierced the horizon the next morning, all the little girl with a red hood could recall seeing was the image of a thousand multi-coloured salamanders with razor-like teeth that revolved inside their mouths rushing out of nowhere to consume the shaman in a silent, bloodless frenzy. Within seconds, the shaman and the salamanders were gone and the girl in red blinked motionlessly for a few seconds before going to the constabulary to inform the startled peon of her discovery. That very night, the poor girl transformed into her own grandmother, never to have to make the treacherous journey across town through the woods fearing for the safety of her chastity, only to finally realise that it was her own kin who had coveted her assets all along. The synthesis of treachery, virtue and greed was so overwhelming that a bastardy new creature appeared in town the next day. It had a withered old woman's face on the body of a wolf that walked upright and had a flap of crimson fur that extended out of its back that billowed when the wind blew or when it was running in full flight.

The ancient tome in question was picked up by the Prince who visited the storehouse of the constabulary after the series of bizarre incidents. The guards in charge of the storehouse were glad to be rid of it, for they believed that the book was the cause of the recent strange occurrences in Keltulop. His status allowed him access and he used it to his advantage. Having been tutored by the five masters of the languages of the world since he was a child, the Prince had little trouble unlocking the secrets between the reddish-brown leather covers of the ancient book. The discovery of its power so enthralled him that he did not leave his room in the castle tower for half a year.

The Prince was not the blood son of the King of Keltulop. The King never had a child with all his seven wives. Save for his last one, all his wives had died by the time the Prince wandered into Keltulop. He was barely five years old when he mysteriously appeared at the city gates. No one knew where he came from except that they could tell from his appearance that he was the offspring of a half man, half minotaur-like creature. He was born with pale, pasty skin and had three eyes – the third eye being located unfortunately on his chin, right under the centre of his lower lip. This eye functioned independently of his two other normal eyes, allowing him to give the impression that he was awake while sleeping. He was also born with horns like that of a bull. However, the horns were not made of bone but of cartilage. As a young child, he took a liking to the soft horns, pulling at them like a child would pull his hair. His birth mother, however, cut them off with a pair of scissors and burned the remaining stumps so that the cartilage-horns would never reappear. This incident conditioned him to hate his own appearance. Other than his dirty, tattered clothes, all he had on him was a torn, brownish parchment found in his pants pocket when he showed up at Keltulop. It wrote that his mother was a slave girl from a city obliterated by the scorching breath of an ocean dragon. The guards at Keltulop's city gate threw the young, grotesque-looking boy into the city gaol as he

---

did not have any travel document on him. For weeks, the boy did not speak. No one could get anything out from him. He looked at everyone blankly and neither shook his head nor made any attempt to communicate verbally or otherwise.

Word of the unsightly boy with obscure origins got to the King and his seventh wife. When the Queen asked the King to take the boy in as their adopted son, the King was livid. He, of royal bearing, would be humiliated and ridiculed for having such a hideous creature as a member of his royal family. But his wife begged him to take the boy in. The royal couple have been trying for a child for years. The King was spectacularly unable to bring forth new brood from his loins. Six wives before the current one and all his bedroom efforts had fallen flat. All of the King's maidens (including the reigning Queen) were pretty, healthy and young when they were inducted into the royal household. As such, the talk in the kingdom have always been the King's infertility. His wives must have died because of his relentless quest every night to sire his new generation. His people whispered to each other how quickly each new queen would become haggard and sallow after being inducted into the royal household. Soon, they would stop appearing in public and then before long, the palace would announce that the queen had died. This pattern persisted with the 70-year-old King and it was with great reluctance that the current queen's father, a simple, unambitious blacksmith, agreed to give away his young daughter to the King in marriage. Fair-skin with luscious, long dark hair, she was only seventeen when the aged King entered her after she entered the palace. It has been half a year since their royal nuptials when the boy from nowhere showed up.

The queen was tired of being the monarch's nightly experiments. She never enjoyed their conjugal activities, not least because of the huge gulf between their ages. She knew what she was getting herself into when she agreed to become the next queen. What else could she have hoped for? As she sat on the cold stone bench just outside her father's blacksmithery after he broke the news to her of the King's request, she looked at both her palms.

They were darkened with soot from helping out at her father's workshop. It was either a lifetime of being a blacksmith's daughter, and then the wife of a man with another menial job, or becoming a blue blood by marriage to the King. Those hands could be filled with jewels, gems and gold. They could remain soft and supple from the nourishment that life in the palace would provide or turn coarse and wrinkled from toiling day and night for the rest of her life with men that ruled over implements and not people. Yet, she knew that she would be no more than a baby making machine even if she chose the former. She asked herself if she has someone special in her heart. It broke her to know that no boy has yet to take his place in it. And so, the decision was clear to her. Saying yes to the arrangement would mean a better life for her father and mother (a royal dowry would see her parents through till they enter their graves without having to work another day for the rest of their lives) and herself. It was a materialistic decision, not one made out of love for the King. If there was any love in the agreement, it was Arconova's love for her parents that guided her to make up her mind.

After her pleas to the King to take in the nameless boy fell on deaf ears for many nights, Queen Arconova became desperate. One night, when the King tried to resume his nocturnal endeavours to create a new blood line, the Queen ran to the edge of the balcony of the royal bedroom. She threatened to throw herself into the moat of water serpents at the bottom of the tower if the King still could not find it in his heart to rescue the boy from the city gaol. Why can't they adopt him, rehabilitate him and educate him to become a member of the royal household? After all, he did not have a past that will complicate ties with any other kingdom since the boy was of unknown origin. The thought of his people starting yet another rumour of him and the royal household felt more loathsome than adopting the ugly creature as his son. A suicide, of their queen no less, would be disastrous for his image. Even his allies would mock him.

A few nights later, ten men from the King's personal guard would be murdered after being poisoned. After taking their last meal after midnight, they became weak and fell to their knees. The King himself, wrapped in a dark cloak, came from behind and executed them one by one with his longsword. Just a few hours ago, the men were tasked with breaking the boy from nowhere out from the gaol and delivering him to the palace. They were sworn to secrecy and promised handsome rewards for the mission. After the boy was safely sent to the palace (and having taken a detour to avoid detection), the men were told to take their supper in the royal kitchen. The King had personally prepared a meal of buffalo innards and bread for his secret warriors. Yet, he laced them with dark weed powder. It was known for generations that dark weed, which were harvested from the delta at the river mouth where the city's river meets the sea, made men weak and could even immobilise them for hours when given in huge quantities. No one should ever know that the King has a son who was in fact the strange, grotesque boy from nowhere.

For many years after that secretive night, no one saw the queen or the boy. The King must keep them out of sight for a few years before formally announcing that he finally has an heir. When he formally introduced them to his people, he explained that the mother and son were both sick and their lives were in danger for many years due to a difficult pregnancy. He was reluctant to break the good news to them because they might die at any moment and that would break their hearts. To protect them, the King said, he sacrificed his royal privileges and had to live a quiet, secluded live for the past decade before he could be sure that both mother and son would continue to live without any danger. He even had the royal physician to corroborate his statement by reading a scripted speech to his people on the same occasion to prove their frailty and the wisdom of the King's difficult decision. By then, the King was old and frail. His people could see the nakedness of his truth as he stood high above them on the royal podium in the centre of the market square. They could see the mismatch between the Prince's announced age (the King said he was ten) and his apparent age (the people could tell that he was more like fifteen or sixteen). Well, maybe the Prince appeared older than he was given the King's inferior ability to sire new brood and his advanced age, giving rise to an offspring who looked less youthful. The shepherds see that in farm dogs, don't they? It was in this way that the masses reconciled the conflict. No one believed in the royal, official version wholesale. Yet, what other explanations could there be?'"

Prince, by Any Other Appearance

Twisted listened and thought to himself that Ngurunguur's latest yarn had the potential to develop into an epic if nothing was done to stop him. Ngurunguur cannot be allowed to go on and on with the story of the ugly boy from nowhere who became a prince. Yet, at the same time, Twisted cannot help but feel a connection with this new character conceived by his rival. After being ostracised in the mortal world by his tribe, Twisted was alone, lonely and desperate. At first, he was simply shunned by everyone and he left his home village. A few weeks later, he tried to return and to seek forgiveness. He was willing to become a slave to everyone in the village, to be at their beck and call. But the thought of him living in the village with a proper roof over his head was too much for the villagers to stomach. The braves, women young and old, even children – they all went after him with whatever implements they could lay their hands on. Even though Twisted ran for his life, it was not difficult to catch him as he was weak from poor nutrition while out in the forest alone. He was dragged back to the village by his hair and dumped in a cage before he was killed. Like the Prince, he was a creature that no one cared about. While the Prince was seen to be hideous on the outside, Twisted was perceived to be ugly inside. Both were deemed grotesque by everyone. As Ngurunguur's plot unfolded, Twisted felt compelled to contribute, too. His desire to be part of this story stemmed more from his empathy towards the character and less from the need to rival Ngurunguur in front of the Devil. And so Twisted intercepted Ngurunguur before he could continue telling the same tale:

"The greatest joy in the world is to be loved. And love was a luxury the Prince had never experienced. He knew that he was unlovable in his natural state. Even a half-man, half-minotaur can be admired for its awesome physique. Yet, he had neither the awe-inspiring, brutish physicality of a minotaur or the refined gracefulness of a man. The Prince was nothing but a tragic mix of blood lines that should never have been allowed to mix. Having been hidden from sight until the King's formal announcement of his existence, the Prince had never been amongst people. Even after that, his contact with fellow human beings were limited to the imperial tutors and servants. Now, in a matter of weeks, he had to attend a soirée. The Prince noticed that his tutors and servants looked at him differently from when they looked at each other. With his severely limited experience in human interaction and behaviour, he could not really understand why it was so. It was not until one day when a servant excitedly called everyone into the royal barn that the Prince finally knew the nature of the look they gave him whenever they saw him. He remembered clearly that it was a weekday morning, just after the morning meal, when the girl servant made the frantic and excited call to get them to see the birth of a new calf in the barn. It was a sight that no one would forget. One of the cows died after giving birth to a calf. It was an unusual offspring – the newborn had only half a face (the left side was missing) and it lay flat on its stomach instead of trying to stand with its yet-to-be tested baby legs. Instead, the calf's legs extended from its back, their hooves pointing towards the roof of the barn. Even more incredulous was the fact that those legs had no knees. Its creator did a bad job and simply impaled stiff, pike-like legs onto its back. It was simply a confusing sight. The Prince looked at everyone's faces and saw a mixture of shock, disgust and ultimately comic disbelief. Indeed, after accepting the fact that what they were seeing was real, the audience in the barn broke into giggles and laughter. It did not matter to them that the calf was tragically designed. It was only a visual spectacle, albeit an unusually bizarre one, to them. It would cause no interruption in their lives despite its almost demonic peculiarity. After talking about it excitedly for a few minutes, everyone returned to what they were doing before.

From that moment, the Prince finally recognised the look that everyone had on them when he saw them looking at him. His tutors always appeared to be suppressing something on their faces whenever they faced him. It was the same look they had on them in the barn with the poor calf. Except that they did not giggle or laugh. It was an expression of shock at first, then disgust and a continuous attempt to stifle both and finally an aborted giggle. Finally, they became expressionless, having gotten over their basic, natural instinct when looking at something so marvellously repulsive. Over time, those reflexes became minute and almost undetectable as they quickly settle into the neutral and polite state of stoic indifference. After all, he was the King's son even though he looked a lot worse than that sorry, pathetic excuse of a baby cow. Inside, everyone loathed looking at him. Except that they had no choice but to look. They could not simply walk away from him like they did at the royal barn.

That experience at the barn taught the Prince that no one could love him because of the way he looked. To experience love, he would have to apply the dark art he acquired from the book taken into the city by the legendary shaman and morph into something beautiful. With the power of the ancient book now in his hands, he could change to look like whoever and whatever he wanted.

A feminine beauty with long, luscious hair would be hard to resist. So, one night, the Prince summoned the powers he had just learnt from the book brought to Keltulop by the shaman and transformed himself in a purpled hair young woman with sparkling silver eyes. Elated with the result, he hummed a tune while looking out of his window high up on the castle tower. Unknowingly, his efforts attracted the attention of a drunk, off-duty soldier who was on his way back to the barracks. Mesmerised by the Prince's newly transformed appearance, the drunk soldier shouted out to the purple hair royal beauty in the dead of the night. The enamoured soldier made it plain that he wished to lay with the exquisite creature high up in the tower. The Prince then willed his hair to grow longer and longer till it reached the ground, allowing the soldier to use the hair as rope to climb into the Prince's room.

Once he was in the room, the soldier glared at the Prince's avatar, oblivious to the misfortune that was about to befall him. The endless purple tresses crawled and wound themselves around the inebriated soldier, twining around his helpless body. Until the moment when the thousands of hair ends pierced his orifices all at once, the soldier was absolutely delighted to be within smelling distance of such a creature and to be caressed by the sensual extensions of its follicles.

The price of such rare beauty was that the Prince needed to extract the life essence from the soft tissues of men if he was to have the ability to retransform back to his original self. He did not need to kill a man every night for his retransformative powers to work. Each soul provided the power for a few retransformations. But he had to kill them anyway every time to avoid being found out. Another limiting condition was that the beauty could not see sunlight. He would have given anything to learn how to reorder the nature of the universe, making it night forever in order to parade in his avatar all the time. Although he no longer has horns, he would make it a point to transform briefly into a minotaur just before resuming his human form. He wished that he could embrace his lineage and walk among men as a true beast to be feared and admired. But he was too cowardly to do so. Also, he must blend in to hide his powers as well as his ambition. For it was in daylight, among unsuspecting men and women, that he searched for the ultimate power to control night and day among the travellers who passed through Keltulop like the forgotten shaman from Xia.

Before long, the Prince grew complacent during his midnight misdeeds. He no longer saw the need to first lure men with a sweet song from the tower. The long, silky and purple tresses were enough to arouse men's curiosity. He lay out the hair so long that they hanged from his tower window down to the ground below and then stretched across the royal garden at the back and onto the footpath just beyond the low, filmsy wooden fence that separated the garden from the path. If passing men did not spot the bright purple ends in the moonlight, the Prince would send the hair to tickle their ankles. Intrigued, they would then follow the trail to its owner.

One night, a frail servant carrying a small white wooden pail of fresh laundry walked along the footpath near the tower. The Prince had fallen asleep from waiting as it was near dawn and no unfortunate soul has yet to take the hairy bait. The servant was short, standing just under five feet and had eyes accustomed to seeing in the dark. It was a path the servant usually did not take and hence she was more vigilant that night. Seeing the mess of purple hair on the ground, the servant put the pail down to investigate. It led the servant to a small opening in the fence, just big enough for an adolescent to crawl through. The fence seemed to have been punched through from the inside by the ends of a large broom as the wood around the opening had tiny puncture marks. Walking across the royal garden, the servant reached the foot of the tower. Looking skywards, climbing up the tower using the purple rope of hair seemed daunting to the bony servant. But this was something too weird to pass up on. With gritted teeth, the servant made the difficult climb upwards. It was first light when the servant was almost within reach of the tower window. It was at this moment that the Prince woke up and stuck his head out of the window and peered down. As sunlight shone onto his face, he started to revert to his old self. The servant saw the beautiful facade turn. First, the left side of the face, the side closer to the east, lost it shine and the servant could see what appeared to be a blinking half-mole on the chin. Also, the servant thought for a moment that a horn appeared and disappeared on the left side of the creature's head. Appalled by the changing, inexplicable sight, the servant loosened the grip on the hair, which by now was fast receding. From the window of his tower, the Prince caught a glimpse of the servant's pleading eyes just before the poor servant slid down the rope even as it became shorter and shorter by the second. He noticed very quickly that there was something uncommon about those eyes – they were not covered by eyebrows. The servant was less than three feet from the ground when there was no more rope to hold on to. With a slight thud, the servant landed on the buttocks and rolled sideways before recovering. As the servant looked up at the window before fleeing, the image of a three-eyed creature illuminated by sunlight was burnt into memory. The servant will be the only person to ever escape death after seeing and touching the purple hair of the creature.

The Prince was disturbed by that episode. Worried that the plucky servant might reveal the secret of his new appearance to the rest of the world, the Prince was forced to make the dangerous decision of venturing out of the castle tower at night to search for the servant. Several men have disappeared without a trace since the Prince acquired his latest skill a month back, many of them soldiers and workers for important people in the town. Questions have gone unanswered and a sense of dread and fear have started to creep in among the townsfolk. It would be foolish not to do anything. But it could have been too late to nip the problem in the bud anyway, for no one could ever keep mum about such a horrifying episode. The Prince knew he would have to pay for his decision the first night he ventured out of his hiding place to look for the servant. Pandora's box was opened – it was now not a question of if, but when and how.

Disguised by his various transformations, the Prince went to every part of the castle town for a fortnight. To blend in during his investigation of the prostitutes' quarter by the dockyard, he went as a Turk sailor with a face full of beard and whose skin was salty, worn and tanned. To sneak into the houses of aristocrats, he found it most convenient to become a groom, first gaining access to their compound via the stables and then ferreting the servants' lodgings in the dead of the night. The idea of becoming an insect or an animal did occur to him and he tested it one night as a cockroach. He would never repeat this feat again as he narrowly escaped death by turning back into human form just before a crow tried to swoop down on him and make a supper meal out of the royal roach.

He would visit the prostitutes' quarter again and again. Anonymity conferred upon him the euphoria of sexual liberation. Drunkenness, licentiousness and general bawdy behaviour that he could not reveal even a hint of within the stony walls of his castle confines became a sport for him, with the Prince trying to outdo himself with each subsequent visit. He became so drunk one night that he changed his outer form a few times on his way home. An old woman afflicted with insomnia looked out of her bedroom window to witness a naked young girl with small, perky breasts on the street turning into a bald, naked old woman much like herself with sagging bosoms. The startled grandmother's hysterical shrieks led to her sons chasing after the apparition down the street. They did not manage to catch up with the protean Prince as moments before that, the Prince's fancy flight of imagination turned him into a swallow that flew him back to his warm bed.

It did not take long before the marketplace and bars in town were filled with incredulous stories. It was feared that the shaman of Xia had brought with him spirits from the mysterious Far East. Evil beings could have followed him throughout his travels and the shaman's ability to call up spirits could mean that they now have nowhere to go after their owner's disappearance. A well-read storyteller related the ancient Chinese folklore of fox spirits as being consistent with the old woman's sighting of the transformation of a young woman into a haggard old woman. The fox spirit uses the physical beauty of young women to attract men to sustain their physical human form. In actuality, they are but ugly animals when they do not disguise their real, devilish selves. This version was popular among the womenfolk who hoped to deter their husbands' wandering hearts from venturing out at night for the men might risk having their souls consumed by the fox spirits as part of the creatures' attempts to further perfect their human form. Another version started to gain currency soon after. The origin of this later version was murky. Some said it was told by members of the constabulary. Others said it was told by a pair of sisters from outside of town. Regardless of the source, this later version spoke of the powers of physical transformation acquired by a member of the royalty. At first, no one knew who it was. The idea of the royalty being possibly embroiled in this greatly excited the townsfolk and tongues started wagging incessantly. The culprit was narrowed down to the Prince due to his mysterious ways. No one could be completely sure, but most were nonetheless convinced that it was the Prince who was responsible for the unexplained sightings of late. The popularity of this version led to disastrous consequences for the Prince's freedom.

To prove the theory posited by the second rumour, people started to camp outside the Prince's tower. It started with a small pack of five or seven vigilantes at night who hoped to catch the Prince red-handed. On the first night that they appeared, the Prince was unaware. Under the cover of darkness, his hair crept down the tower and crawled silently onto the footpath. To his surprise, he felt the ankles of not one but several men. Shocked, he slowly withdrew his hairy tentacles. Looking out of the window into the darkness, he did not see anybody. He then turned himself into a crow, flying himself out of the tower window before landing on a tree branch. There, he transformed into a snake and slithered down the tree trunk nearer to the ground. From about a height of five feet from the ground, he could spot a few men seated on the side of the footpath with their heads turned up towards his tower. His first reaction was rage. He had almost wanted to turn into a giant boa to strangulate all of them at once. But just before he did so, he realised the foolishness of that thought as it would prove once and for all that the Prince had something to do with the disappearances. Sanity restored, he slowly crept back to his tower in the form of a small, simple tree snake that he chose to masquerade as. That night, he sat up in bed unable to sleep. Deprived of opportunities to extract men's life essence, he could only morph into creatures of a lower order, like reptiles and insects, as he did not need too much effort to revert to his original form. But to turn himself back from a beautiful woman, that required extra effort which only the energy stored in the souls of men could provide. He was to spend several nights that followed thinking about his new problem as the few men from the initial night was to swell into a mess of a crowd having a midnight mass picnic outside his tower. More men appeared out of curiosity and days later, womenfolk and children started to join the ranks. One night, the hysterical granny who sparked off the rumour mill showed up too. Her sons and grandsons took turns to piggyback her from their house five miles away. Before long, hawkers peddling snacks and drinks appeared so as to profit from the nightly party of rumour seekers. The Prince could only get the King to send out the royal cavalry to disperse the crowd, citing law and order concerns. That strategy only worked for a short while. The crowd merely disappeared for a night or two. Nights later, they would reappear, occupying different spots in the same night as all who showed up thought it would be better to observe the tower from elsewhere. So, instead of removing the problem, policing it only multiplied it. It was not possible to guard everywhere since the pockets of people were constantly changing their positions night after night and quite a number of them chose to park themselves sufficiently far enough from the royal garden for the cavalry to reasonably accuse them of posing a threat. In any case, the hunting ground of the Prince became a hive of activity. The area became too busy for the Prince to prey on anyone.

It was in such circumstances that the Prince was to attend the soirée. He was painfully aware that the occasion would only further degrade him in the eyes of everyone in Keltulop. A royal disgrace he would be. He was neither handsome nor talented by any conventional interpretation. Also, he would have to put up with the scrutiny amidst the latest scandal in town. Yet, he must nevertheless attend to show and reaffirm his father's status among the nobility. He was required to put on a bow tie and a tuxedo for the party. But beyond that, he did not really bother to do anything else. He would just go through the motions and get the night over and done with. There was nothing much to do anyway, not with the crowd outside his tower observing him. As expected, several well-dressed young men and women of royal blood were at the soirée. Many showed off their outstanding abilities in dancing, singing, poetry recital, painting, equestrian, among other aristocratic talents. The Prince, after his formal introduction by the hostess, stood in a corner. He did not expect to be noticed anyway, given that he was ignored all his life. He did not blame anyone. He would not have wanted to talk to himself either. How he wished he could turn himself into that beautiful creature seen by so many men in his room that very instant! But something else happened at that very moment to distract the Prince.

The top of a tall, black hat with several arrows embedded with their fletchings sticking out of the hat literally appeared right under the Prince's flared nostrils. The hat and the fletchings seemed to turn counter clockwise as more of the hat rose up to the level of his eyes. When the sudden, abrupt image finally came to a stop, the Prince saw what he thought to be the back of a head. The Prince nearly let out a horrifying scream when a pair of eyes, a nose and a mouth appeared altogether in a flash on that visage before him. The owner of the facial orifices covered the Prince's gaping mouth with hands that came out of nowhere, stifling the Prince's startled cries. No one was alarmed, except for him. The wearer of the top hat let out a wide grin before rearranging the position of the eyes, nose and even the smiling mouth on the face. It appeared as if a surgeon was trying to determine the perfect location for the orifices in an experiment to find out if there were better places to position them. The Prince by now was more amazed than shocked. He was sure that he was not hallucinating or delirious, for the party so far has been testing the limits of his ability to put up with boredom to the extent that he started to recall mathematical equations that he learnt as a child. He was more logical than ever when the strange image appeared. He has yet to drink any alcohol by then, too. The Prince was trying to make sense of the moving facial features and everything that has gone on so far when the entire head spun round on its shoulders with incredible speed. When it finally stopped spinning after who knows how many rounds, the head bent back and forth a few times before it stopped. This time, the eyes, nose and mouth were all where they should be and they no longer moved about. The Prince was glad that all was static. He did not even realise that the owner of the hat was no longer covering his mouth. The Prince saw that the man had different coloured eyes. The left eye was silver and the right eye was crimson. His hat changed colours when the

Prince tilted his head from side to side trying to ascertain the exact colours of the eyes. Fascinated, the Prince walked around the man, not taking his eyes off him. He expected the man's head to turn and follow him while he walked around. But the man did not move a single muscle at all while the Prince conducted his inspection. With every step around the man, the hat changed colours. It was not a gradual shift in shade or hue. Rather, each colour contrasted sharply against the one before. Red followed black, lime green came after red, gray followed, and then sky blue. The Prince stood in front of the man after completing his round and continued to look intently at the stranger, trying to register and remember everything about this bizarre but wholly interesting being.

'Who are you?' the Prince asked.

'Who do you want me to be?' The man replied as he alternated between cocking his left and right eyebrow.

'You look quite mad to me,' said the Prince, staring at the man from head to toe. Both the sleeves of the man's tuxedo was torn. The right sleeve seemed to be ripped off at the elbow, while the left was frayed a few inches above the wrist. His turquoise pants were baggy, wholly incongruent with the style of the nobility. Thankfully, the pants were not torn as the Prince cannot imagine how much more outlandish the man would look. His footwear shocked the Prince, who at first look thought the man was barefooted. The Prince squat down to investigate further. Touching his foot with his ungloved hands, the Prince felt the coldness of metal and not the warmth of skin. Looking up at the man with the hat that changed colours, the Prince asked what method was used to make the metallic shoes transparent.

'Madman's alchemy,' came the reply.

'Fascinating,' the Prince mumbled to himself several times as he stood up, all the while looking down at the shoes even as he straightened himself. When the Prince finally took his eyes off the shoes, the man started to vanish bit by bit. His head crumbled like sand and poured into the cavity in the neck where the head once was. Both arms were sucked into that same hole, fingers first. The torso then split into two equal vertical halves and each half collapsed into the top of the thigh bones. Finally, the skin on both legs started to develop angry, red boils before bursting into flames. The fire burnt bright orange for a few seconds and abruptly turned into a pale, light blue before being sucked away by a vacuum that seemed to have its source from the ceiling right above the Prince's head. The Prince reached down quickly to grab one of the transparent metal shoe but he was too slow. Everything that belonged to the mad alchemist with the colourful hat was gone. Just as he stood up and looked around for signs of the mad man, an arrow with peacock patterned fletching floated past his face in a surreally slow manner. The arrow was transformed into a full-length peacock feather in mid-flight and its speed increased several times just as the Prince reached out to grab it. But the feather flew just beyond his reach and the Prince hurriedly chased after it. He sprang a few awkward steps forward, both arms outstretched. The feather floated effortlessly amidst the crowd of well-dressed people, indifferent to the importance of the occasion and the anxiety of the Prince. It probably lasted only a few short seconds but the Prince felt intense agitation while on its trail. It ended with the Prince placing his right hand on the left shoulder of another stranger he was to interact with meaningfully that evening."

AND SO, SHE APPEARS

Voice from the Heart was but an ordinary denizen of hell. Unlike Ngurunguur and Twisted, she was no storyteller in her mortal life. There are hundreds of millions, if not billions, like her in the afterworld. All the while as Ngurunguur and Twisted engaged in the contest, Voice from the Heart listened intently. She recalled that the Devil wanted to hear an original tale. Yet, the Devil never said that only those who had been storytellers whilst alive were eligible to engage in the contest. For all her life, Voice from the Heart was never able to truly say what she felt. She was taught from young that girls should always be quiet and never be heard. Be seen, not heard, was the maxim that she was taught to live by. Even if she did speak, instead of saying what she truly thought and felt, she was trained to say the contrary of what was on her mind or in her heart. In this way, she was deemed to be socially acceptable. She remembered clearly that she insisted on staying alone in her family's hut that summer when she died. Her parents and her elder brother made a trip to the market in the big city. It would be a return journey of two weeks. Voice from the Heart heard of all the delights of the city since she was little and yearned to see the bright lights and savour the novel, tasty treats at the nightly bazaars. She could even pick up a new toy or adorn herself with a new fashion accessory or two. But someone had to stay home to watch the hut. They lived next to a swamp in the hot and humid southern tip of the country. Two weeks away would see the hut overrun with all sorts of swamp life – mostly amphibians like frogs, snakes and salamanders, due to the frequent rainfall in their sub-tropical climate in summer. Flooding was common as their part of the country was constantly neglected by the authorities due to its insignificance and backwardness. So, even though it was her dream to see the city, young Voice from the Heart (barely sixteen) denied herself of the opportunity and appeared genuinely not to want to accompany her family. In any case, her family expected her to turn them down anyway. Someone had to stay behind and it had to be her (who else?!).

Death conferred upon her a different life. It liberated her. She was no longer held back by the constraints of mortal society with its perverse, man-made moral codes and norms of behaviour defined by culture. She does not have to fulfil anyone's expectations of her anymore. Why should she? When she stayed behind to tend to the family hut, bandits came by one night. Those bottom feeders had just finished robbing a family in another town several miles away and were on their way back to their hideout. They used a different route to avoid detection and they chanced upon Voice from the Heart's dwelling. Seeing that it was deserted (no one else lived within shouting distance of her hut near the swamp), the bandits crept up to her house in the dead of the night. She was sleeping when the five men looked down at her while she lay on her bed of bamboo matting. They tore her clothes and raped her for hours before killing her. There was nothing much of value to steal. In the morning, the men fled and left her body there for the creatures of the swamp. She should have been in the centre of town strolling around with a bright red lantern and watching strong men perform acrobatic, martial arts feats.

Having been in hell for centuries since, Voice from the Heart listened to thousands of plots and storylines by the dead storytellers around her. Always passive, perennially in the background, now Voice from the Heart was no longer contented to play the quiet listener, to suppress her thoughts when she (like any other normal person dead or alive) has so much to express. Now is her time to say whatever she wants. If she does it right, she has a chance to regain her mortality and live the life she should have. For the first time in her existence both above and below ground, Voice from the Heart spoke up to express herself. She could finally give her input on the nature of man. From where Twisted had briefly stopped, Voice from the Heart began:

"The feather was nowhere to be seen. Instead, the Prince was met by a pair of startled eyes. He found himself looking not at the eyes but the area around it, as if searching for clues to a treasure on a map. Before he could locate a hint of what he was looking for, a soft, female voice interrupted his search.

'What... What do I...?' That was all she could muster.

He expected to see the mad alchemist. But this time, there was none of that irreverence or incoherence. The image before him was that of a young woman without any make-up. Her skin was pale. Her face was dotted with pink freckles and her shoulder-length hair was straight and jet black. There was an air of subservience, of constant, disguised fear about her. She looked down quietly after taking in the manner of the Prince's attire. The girl was wearing a simple white gown with shoulder straps. There were no accessories on her and she wore a pair of plain, white open-toe slippers made out of straw. Just then, before the Prince could make a formal introduction, the Prince's father took to the stage and announced the start of the dance. It was the tradition for all young men and women at the soirée to engage in one dance at the end of the individual performances just before dinner. Almost everyone will make prior arrangements weeks before on their choices of partners as it would have to be mutually consented to. Letters of intent will be written and the to-ing and fro-ing of responses necessitated careful, advanced planning. The Prince was too caught up with settling his own mess to look into this matter. When the orchestra commenced playing swiftly after the King's announcement – everything was planned for and there was little time wasted at these events attended by the nobility, the Prince simply reached out and grabbed the girl with both his hands. He tried to dance using a mixture of skipping from side to side, waltzing forward and backward and turning round in circles, all the time trying to lead the girl into his steps. Neither of them could dance competently or even keep time with the music – the Prince paid scant attention to the dance tutors hired by his mother and the girl was all lost at sea as she had never danced a single step in her life. It was fortunate that they were cast away in a corner of the hall. Only a few guests saw their awful dance as most gathered near the center of the hall to admire the graceful steps of the sons and daughters of the various counts, dukes and barons in attendance. These unfortunate few turned their eyes away in disgust and sought better views elsewhere. The music stopped after some time and the Prince and his dance partner were both relieved. The hapless girl ran away as soon as the dance ended, covering her face with her left hand as she did so. The Prince hurried after her but he soon lost sight of her as she meandered her way among the many bodies amassed on the dance floor. He did not want to be seen by others to be flustered or be kicking up a fuss. So, he retreated to another corner of the hall and waited for dinner to be served.

Dinner was to be a drab affair. Seated between and among people who eyed him suspiciously, the Prince pretended to be a member of the esteemed crowd, dining with extreme etiquette and behaving as royally as he was trained to be. But in his mind, he played with images of himself torturing all those random men who fell victim in his tower all those nights. When he had exhausted his memory of those nights, he started to think of the mad alchemist and the young woman with no name. Both fascinated him great-ly. The mad alchemist was thoroughly ridiculous while the young woman captivated the Prince with her sadness and plain beauty. He was to become more preoccupied with her as the evening wore on. As he ate his dinner at the long table with great care outwardly, the Prince's mind raced haphazardly to conjure theories of who the freckled girl was and how she had ended up at the soirée. He had never before danced with a female of his age. All his dance experi-ences were with his dance tutors or their assistants and they were all decades his senior. The girl's shyness and her hidden fear – of what the Prince did not know, greatly aroused the Prince's curiosity. He was quite sure she was not a member of the elite because of her dressing. Even some one as ugly as the Prince was well-attired just because he was an invited member and a participant of the soirée. He was there to be formally introduced to and inducted into the aristocracy. She cannot be one of them. More clues pointed to this conclusion – her dancing, or lack of it, and her ignorance of royal etiquette. Even with poor dance sense like the Prince's, there would be some attempts to fall back to a few basic steps simply due to the many hours spent on drills supervised by teachers. Instead, the Prince felt as if he was trying to pull a deaf and blind donkey with three legs to follow him rhythmically. Furthermore, she did not even bother to introduce herself even if she had to rush off at the end of the dance. Who then, could she be?

He found the answer after dinner. Once dessert – it was pudding with sheeps' eyes, was over, the Prince skipped out of the stifling confines of the dining hall and went out onto the porch to enjoy the cool Keltulop evening air. The full moon shone brightly in the clear sky. As the Prince looked around the porch, he spotted a lone figure sitting alone by the bench next to the statue of Alice the Wonder. He walked over and to his surprise and joy, it was the girl he danced with a few hours ago. He tried to start off with a few lines on the origins of the statue but his plan was abruptly and unexpectedly interrupted by a woman's shouts.

'Get here, you!'

It was followed quickly by 'Cinderella, now!'

The young girl in the cheap, white dress got up from the bench and dashed off immediately upon hearing those words uttered by two different women. She almost knocked over the Prince in her haste. She ran away so fast that the Prince was still in a muddle over what to do. He felt that going after her would reveal too starkly his intentions. Yet, he felt an overriding impulse to give chase. In any case, he was rooted to the spot while he deliberated on the desired course of action. The girl was long gone by then and the Prince muttered to himself, 'Cinderella'. He looked at where she was seated moments ago and wished he had skipped dessert and came out onto the porch much earlier. But he was not without reward. He saw the pair of open-toed slippers that belonged to Cinderella on the ground under the bench. She must have forgotten to wear them in her mad dash. He picked them up and inspected them closely. Running his fingers through the weave of its toe straps, he discovered that they were made of grass and yet they were white. On closer look, the colour was off-white, with hues of gray at some parts. They appeared white under the strong lighting of the dance hall. But under the moon's natural, softer shine, the understated shades of the slippers became more apparent. The Prince clutched the slippers with both hands in front of his chest and walked back to the party. The moon overhead cast a sly grin of the Cheshire cat."

About Her

Voice from the Heart paused, cleared her throat and cast a sidelong glance at Twisted. She was not sure why she did so because she had no intention of stopping even if he showed any adverse reaction to her participation in the contest. She knew very well that it was not just Twisted who was questioning her credentials and eligibility. An unknown, insignificant soul like her numbered in the billions in the Devil's sanctum of death. Who was she to try to wrest the prize away from seasoned bards like Ngurunguur and Twisted? But Voice from the Heart had waited more than a lifetime to speak up. She was not going to give up now just because of censuring looks cast her way. Looking ahead at the infinite gathering of souls before her, Voice from the Heart continued her tale of the futility of changing one's fate:

"The villagers clapped and cheered when the toothless crocodile pulled the baby from the foot of the ash heap hill. The keeper of the crocodile was a strange, mysterious old woman. Nobody ever saw her face as she covered herself from head to toe with a black cloth. Some said she was blind and needed the reptile to guide her around her swamp dwelling. No one ever got close enough to peer under her hood to see her eyes because of the creature. Getting caught in the crocodile's vice-like grip was painful even if there was no rotten ivory lining those powerful jaws. All anyone could discern was that she had some sort of growth on her back, giving her the appearance of a hunched back. That morning, the woman and her pet guide emerged unexpectedly on a clear Sunday morning from the swamp at the edge of the riverine settlement and cut across the marketplace. Children were startled and the villagers were unnerved. She had never appeared when the sun was up. As the feared duo lumbered across the marketplace, everyone including the warriors who protected the place from invaders gingerly lined themselves in neat rows to make way for them and watched quietly. When they finally made it to the other side of the marketplace, they exited the settlement and headed towards the hills where rubbish from the village were dumped. Curious – for the woman was not bringing anything with her except the reptile, the villagers quietly and timidly followed.

For centuries, villagers from the settlement would cart their garbage and dump them at the foot of the barren hills. Every month, a large fire would be lit to destroy the rubbish left there. It was also a practice to throw enemies captured from battles into the fire. Condemned prisoners met with the same fate, too. Over time, a heap of ash appeared there. It was almost as tall as the hills themselves. Wind never blew in that desolate place and rain had never fallen there either. When the woman and her crocodile travelled to the hill that morning, it was weeks before the start of another bonfire. She had no reason to go there.

When she got to the ash heap hill, she bent down to touch the snout of the reptile and released her grip on the leash. The crocodile then ventured on its own. It circled round the foot of the hill, poking and sniffing as it did so. It was to do so for an hour before it finally focused all its attention on a particular spot. It turned around and used its tail to lash wildly at that spot for a long time. When it finally stopped, it turned and started to use its snout to push into the space it had created. It stopped moving for several minutes and the onlookers thought it was dead. The old woman never moved throughout. She simply sat and waited. Some of the villagers wanted to go up to her to tell her that her pet had died and they should head back home before dark. Just as they wanted to do so, the reptile moved back with much effort. Slowly pushing itself backwards with all its limbs, the crocodile had within its jaws both legs of a baby. It eventually pulled the entire baby from the ash heap and turned to face its owner. Amidst the cheering and disbelieving cries of the villagers, the woman walked to her pet and retrieved the baby gently from its jaws. With the gray, ash covered infant in her arms, the old woman walked up to the village chief. As she did so, she placed the baby face down on her right arm and gently patted the baby's back with her left hand. The tiny new life coughed violently a few times, spewing out small clouds of ash as it did so. The woman then handed the baby to the village chief with outstretched arms. Once the baby was safely with the village chief, the woman walked back to her crocodile. She knelt in front of its snout and pried open its jaws with both hands. To the villagers' horror, the old woman crawled into the reptile's jaws and disappeared inside the creature. Then, the crocodile leapt twenty feet skywards. At the zenith of its jump, it turned and nosedived with tremendous speed towards the ground. As it crashed onto the ground, it created a hole upon impact and vanished inside and below the soil. Those on the surface could make out that the reptile was tunnelling its way back towards her owner's swamp settlement through the unevenness and bumps created in the ground just below the surface. The next morning, warriors who scouted the swamp reported that a lush, fertile field had taken the place of the putrid wetland. In one corner of the field was a small cottage. The cottage was empty, except for a small, wooden desk. On the desk was a sealed envelope addressed to the village chief.

From that day onwards, the village chief took care of the baby. He named her Cinderella. No one could be sure why he agreed to it as his wife had given birth to twin girls just two years ago. The contents of the letter was never seen by anyone else. It appeared that the village chief treated Cinderella as his own as he did not show any favouritism during their tender years. But after Cinderella was twelve, it became clear that she would not have equal standing. Cinderella had to tend to her adopted sisters' every need. She made their meals, washed their clothes, cleaned up after them and was at their beck and call. She did everything that was asked of her without complaining. But that was not enough. Cinderella was a fast, diligent worker who learnt quickly. Seeing how she was handling her chores and duties proficiently, her adopted mother and sisters would invent acts of cruelty just for their own amusement.

The morning after her twelfth birthday, Cinderella was hauled out of bed by her adopted mother when the sun rose. The young girl had no idea what was going on as the older woman dragged her out of her bed by her arms and led her rather violently to the backyard. She was placed on a stool in the middle of the backyard. Beside her were a tub filled with water, a pile of soiled clothes and a brush made from the hairs of hedgehogs. Wash, she was told. With that command, Cinderella was to spend the next four hours trying to do something she had never done before. She had seen Kreeta the housemaid doing household chores before that day. But from then on, Kreeta did not exist in that household anymore; Cinderella will take over Kreeta's role. Her tiny hands with the untested skin cracked from using the harsh brush. Like a mule, she did what she was told without any question. There was no one to complain to in any case as her adopted mother and sisters did not step into the backyard before the washing was done. She hanged the clothes to dry after washing everything. As she was not as tall as Kreeta, Cinderella had much difficulty doing so. Jumping, she would try to hang each item of clothing over the clothing lines that were at least four heads higher than her. That whole process of washing and drying took up the entire morning. When she was done, she stepped back into the house. Famished and on the verge of fainting for she had not eaten breakfast, she took a loaf of bread from the kitchen table. Just then, her adopted mother and sisters appeared at the kitchen door. Her adopted mother walked up to her briskly and dragged her out into the backyard by her left arm. In such haste, Cinderella almost dropped the loaf of bread and had to quickly leave it on a side table before stepping out into the backyard. Once in the backyard, Cinderella watched as her adopted family rummaged through the washed laundry. Each item of clothing was picked and scrutinised. In her innocence, Cinderella did not know what was going on. Finally, after a good fifteen minutes or so, her mother and sisters took a handful of clothes, mostly white-based ones, and dangled them in front of Cinderella. They pointed out the stains and spots that

remained despite her washing. Once they made their point, the se-
lected clothes were thrown onto the ground and they stepped back
inside the house. Cinderella stared down at the small pile of clothes
next to her feet. She felt small and her head started to spin. She was
already weak from not having eaten since she had woken up. The
new situation of her young life started to overwhelm her and she
started to weep. As she dried her nose and eyes with her forearms and
palms, Cinderella knelt down to pick up the clothes and proceeded
to wash them again. This time, she paid extra attention to the stains
and spots that she had missed earlier. Before she hanged them up to
dry, she carefully inspected each of them again by holding them up
against the sunlight that mercilessly shone on her that summer day.
She checked every sleeve, every collar, every lapel, flipping them over
several times to make sure that they were spotless. By the time she
finished, it was already mid-afternoon. When she went back into the
kitchen to eat something, she sat down with the loaf of bread and
bit into a slice that she cut for herself. Tears started to flow down her
cheeks as she ate and her first slice of plain bread that day tasted of
salt as she ate silently. She was later found unconscious by the village
chief on the kitchen floor holding on to a slice of half eaten bread.

Cinderella was quick to adjust to her new situation. There was
no one to turn to. Even her stepfather the village chief was nonchalant to Cinderella's plight. He did nothing that night he found
her on the kitchen floor. The dinner arrangement that same night
confirmed to Cinderella her new status – she sat separately from
them by the kitchen door that led to the backyard while the rest of
her adopted family ate as usual in the living room. That dinner was
painful to Cinderella as she quietly sobbed and ate her tear-stained
dinner of half cooked potatoes and lentils. That would be a dinner
she would never forget; as she ate, she bitterly vowed to bear the
future and the unpleasantness that would ensue quietly. Years later,
when asked why she did not choose to run away or even kill her
adopted family, Cinderella explained simply that it was the natural order of things for some to be controlled while others did the
controlling. 'The ox bears no grudge against the cart that it pulls,'
Cinderella would say as she lay dying on her bed.

The next morning, Cinderella assumed her role as the housemaid willingly. She rose at 4am and made breakfast for everyone. Her adopted family was quietly shocked that Cinderella did so without being ordered to or coerced. That second day of her new life went by smoothly, mostly because her stepmother and stepsisters were still trying to grasp Cinderella's almost miraculous adaptability and resilience. Cinderella was the perfect housemaid. Everything that Kreeta used to do – from cooking, washing, cleaning, to minding everything big and small like collecting firewood, Cinderella took over seamlessly. She accepted her fate. But her adopted family would not settle at that. The task of complicating Cinderella's life would fall on her stepmother and stepsisters, with the village chief condoning the acts that followed through his non-intervention.

That Friday morning, the elder sister Celia pretended to be sick. While the rest were eating breakfast out in the living room, Celia lay in bed. Unknown to Cinderella, Celia took ash collected by her sister Delia and herself the previous evening and used it to soil all the bedsheets in the house. After breakfast, Celia made a complaint to her mother about the dirt. It was surmised that the dirt must have been the cause of Celia's illness. Cinderella went about removing the bedsheets in all the rooms without being asked. Neither did she enquire about the origins of the dirt. She spent a large part of the morning after breakfast washing the dirty sheets and hanging them out to dry. The sheets dried quickly under the hot summer sun. Before nightfall, Cinderella was able to collect them and make the bed for everyone just in time. It was an uneventful night. But just before dawn, a loud scream was heard and woke everyone up. Cinderella was well awake by then, having risen at 4am like the day before to prepare breakfast. A commotion took place in Celia's room which she shared with her sister. Celia complained of a terrible nightmare in which she was surrounded by a heavy scent of smoke. She said she felt dizzy and was unable to breathe well upon waking up. Her mother did a quick inspection of the bed and found the underside of Celia's pillow to be stained with gray ash. Cinderella could not believe her eyes as her stepmother held the offending pillow to her face. To make matters worse, Delia brought out a bucket of stones from under Cinderella's bed almost gleefully. Cinderella swore to herself that she had never before seen that bucket. She would know as she swept the floor every day. Her accusers drew the link between the ash under Celia's pillow to the pebbles under Cinderella's bed. Charges of witchcraft were thrown at her. Her stepmother and stepsisters said that Cinderella had placed a hex on Celia. Everyone concurred that her resentment with household chores drove Cinderella to commit such evil acts. Her punishment was to kneel on tiny seashells under the hot midday sun. Also, her eyebrows would be shaved. Her stepmother said that this was a method used to stop young witches from acquiring more potent powers. That afternoon, Cinderella could not decide which hurt more – to be accused of being a witch or the sharp edges of the shells against her knees. When the sun finally set after a long summer day, she rose from her ordeal to make dinner for the family hurriedly. They sat around and waited while Cinderella prepared dinner all by herself. Tired from her punishment and hard pressed for time, she burnt her hands while trying to handle a pot using a piece of cloth that was too thin. She almost let the pot drop to the floor but held on to it when she thought about how she had to be the one to clean up the kitchen floor of spilled stew. The thin cloth provided little protection. She dipped her hands into a pail of cold water after she painfully settled the pot safely on the kitchen floor. The next morning, both her palms grew red and they stung when she tried to clench her fists. For the next two weeks, she used the lower part of her forearms to carry heavy objects as she could not close either hand without bringing tears to her eyes.

When she recovered, she could finally get fresh water from the well just outside the village marketplace. She tried very hard not to use up the water stored at home during the two weeks that she was injured. But that summer was one of the hottest in recent times and it caused a drought. The village wells had all but dried up and Cinderella gathered only half a pail of water from three wells located in different parts of the village. That would not last them more than a day. Her stepmother and stepsisters had started to take more baths every day since the hot spell began. Their needs must be met, or else. That night, Cinderella decided to collect water from the stream next to the castle in Keltulop. The town was a good three-mile walk from her village. She planned to first collect two buckets of fresh drinking water from the stream and then return to the stream to wash dirty laundry in the same night. That way, the water supply at home would last longer. So, she set off after dinner to perform these tasks. Whenever she left the house, she had to wear a standard attire that consisted of a light blue tunic, black pants and an inverted V-shaped three-cornered hat that almost covered her eyes. This was a rule set by the village chief. He did not really favour letting her venture beyond the house. But as his wife and daughters have gotten used to dumping all menial labour and chores to Cinderella, it was unavoidable that Cinderella had to be allowed to leave the house from time to time.

In the darkness of the night, no one could tell clearly who she was, much less her gender. She set off to the stream with two empty buckets once she cleaned up after dinner. She filled the buckets almost to the brim. But she realised that she overestimated her physical ability to carry them back. They felt heavier than what she had thought as she did not factor in the three-mile walk on paths that alternated between rocky and sandy. By the time she reached home, both buckets had each lost almost a fifth of the water collected due to spillage. She felt a little exasperated but there was no other choice. Her night was far from over, though. Cinderella collected the dirty laundry and went back to the stream with an empty wooden pail. By the time she had finished washing laundry at the stream, it was almost dawn. She quickly set about making her way back home, hoping to reach just after first light to prepare breakfast. In her haste to get home quicker, Cinderella took a short cut. She thought she could be faster by half an hour using that route. Instead of using the major path taken by most that passed by cottage huts, storehouses and stations maintained by the royal guards, she tried to cut across a forested area that would bring her right beside the garden below the Prince's tower. With her eyes used to seeing in the dark from waking up just before dawn to prepare breakfast, Cinderella trod carefully, trying to avoid potholes and other potential hazards on the unfamiliar path. It was there, right next to the Prince's lair that she spotted the trap laid by him. Despite being hard pressed for time, her curiosity got the better of her. Minutes later, when she landed on the grass patch at the foot of the tower, Cinderella still had the presence of mind to retrieve her pail of freshly washed laundry before fleeing home.

She arrived home just in time to hastily prepare breakfast. Despite her traumatic episode, Cinderella was able to suppress her fright and concentrate on performing her duties. Her adopted family did not notice anything amiss with their child-servant. She washed her soiled tunic and pants after lunch and dried them under the scorching sun. At night, she willed herself to travel to the stream again to fetch water. Cinderella planned to make two trips as the amount she brought back earlier would not see them through the week. She resolved not to take the short cut no matter what. Also, she decided to wear Delia's clothes without her stepsister's knowledge since the whole family would be sound asleep when she set off in the dead of the night. Cinderella feared that the frightful creature may recognise her if she wore the same clothes. Tired from not having slept for a night, Cinderella paced herself for two return journeys and she was careful not to spill too much water and not to be seen by anyone or anything. It was a comparatively uneventful journey and she was relieved. Having accomplished her mission, she was grateful to get to sleep for a few hours before dawn.

Cinderella was not to wake up till two full days later. Her fatigue was compounded by fright and they combined to give her a rest fraught with bad dreams and a fever. In her dreams, she was harassed by a bull in different scenarios. Sometimes, she dreamt of being captured by a bull that stood erect on its hind legs. Holding her with its front legs, the bull spun round and round, laughing aloud at the same time. Other times, she would be chased by a gigantic bull that would turn itself into a huge boulder and rolled after her. Cinderella developed a high fever. The warmer she became, the more intense the dreams were and a sense of doom overcame her in her fitful sleep. In her delirium, she started talking in her sleep. When her sleep talking first began, Cinderella spouted words at random. No one could contextualise what 'hair', 'rope', 'castle tower', 'monster' and 'horn' meant when Cinderella uttered them in no recognisable order. Curious, the twin sisters tried to talk to Cinderella. It was out of sheer boredom that Delia and Celia experimented with the interrogation since they did not do much work in the house. They were shocked when they realised that Cinderella was caught in a semi-conscious state, floating between sleep delirium and being conscious enough to respond to verbal stimuli.

It started with Delia asking 'What monster?'.

'Castle tower. Monster there,' came the reply. Delia's eyes grew incredulously large. She ran to get Celia and informed her twin of the discovery.

The twin sisters then spent the next few hours sitting by Cinderella's bedside to try to tease out more information. It was the longest time the sisters have ever gotten close to Cinderella since the day she became their de facto housemaid. The sisters tried their best to extract from Cinderella enough clues to piece together a consistent narrative. The more they tried to pin down the sleeping maid, the more confusing it became for them.

'Were there hairs on the horns?'

'Who kept the ropes in the castle?'

'Did all the bulls have horns? Or was it only one that had horns?'

Never once did Cinderella give a reply in the affirmative or negative. Rather, she went on muttering words that were tangential to the sisters' questions. In their excitement, the sisters did not pick up on that to change their tact. Such questions and the inevitable non-replies from Cinderella kept the sisters going in circles.

The only consistent utterance from Cinderella was to associate the castle tower with a monster. She kept saying 'monster, castle tower' every now and then regardless of the different questions posed to her. Exhausted, all the sisters could conclude was that Cinderella was having a very long and bad dream about a frightful creature in a castle tower.

When she finally woke up, Cinderella was disoriented. She could not recall what her daily routine was. Her stepmother and stepsisters thought that Cinderella was putting on an act by using illness as an excuse to avoid performing household chores. For a week, they punished Cinderella over and over again due to her oversights – like not washing the laundry on time, not preparing meals or cleaning the floor. It was uncharacteristic of Cinderella the housemaid to repeat the same infractions over several days despite being made to kneel on seashells in the open under the hot sun or stand on one leg on a stool while balancing a cup filled with water placed on her head for hours on end. This was not the same Cinderella. She seemed to have lost the ability to remember her duties and she even dread being punished. Her adopted family concluded that Cinderella was not acting out of sorts because she was defiant. The new Cinderella appeared lost, rudderless and wholly incapable of reflection. Her step family wondered what happened to the stoic, quick learner who adjusted rapidly to anything that was thrown at her. After a week of Cinderella not performing up to par as the house maid, the house was in a semi-chaotic state. There was not enough clean water for cooking and drinking. They almost ran out of fresh clothes to change into as Cinderella was not tending to the dirty laundry. Meals were often served late and the food tasted bad. Cinderella was getting punished too often for her to be effective in carrying out her duties even if she remembered what they were at all. By the end of the week, there was not enough food in the pantry to serve even a spartan dinner.

Dismayed and frustrated by the condition of the house and their servant, the stepmother and stepsisters were finally made to lift their fingers to alleviate their near-calamitous situation. For the first time in months, they had to venture to the market to purchase produce and groceries. It was there that they first hear about the gossip of the latest strange on-goings in Keltulop. The village was administered by Keltulop and its marketplace was frequented by the townsfolk from Keltulop who found the ashen-style pottery of the village exotic. Almost everyone was exchanging what they knew about the mysterious disappearances. The twin sisters overheard bits and pieces of the news from shop owners and patrons alike. Curious, they enquired as much as they could. Keltulop and its surrounding villages did not witness much excitement. Save for the shaman of Xia's spectacular vaporisation and the appearance and then disappearance of the hunchback woman and her crocodile, it was a humdrum existence for most folks there. The stepmother and her daughters were quickly brought up to speed by the butcher's wife and the elderly shopkeeper who sold them oats and bread. The shopkeeper's son served in the royal constabulary and one of his comrades had been missing for several days. The old man told the mother and the twins of the feared fox spirits and warned them to keep a close eye on the village chief, lest he becomes besotted by one of the spirits and then go on to lose his soul. The stories that they heard intrigued them. Just before leaving the marketplace, the three women walked past a painter who was putting the finishing touches to a water colour depiction of a face. It showed a two-faced creature whose right side was that of a beautiful girl with long flowing hair. The other side was the face of a horned demon with a terrifying, bloodshot eye. The painter noticed the interest of the women and he offered to give it to them for free if they helped him to choose the colour of the girl's hair since he had a long time debating with himself what colour to use. Delia picked up a brushed and dipped it in blue ink. Seeing her twin taking action, Celia did not want to lose out. So, Celia took a different brush and dipped it in red ink as she did not want to be accused of not being original. As both sisters started to enthusiastically colour the girl's long, flowing hair, the colours were liberally mixed on the canvas to produce an inconsistent interpretation of purple that got lighter the farther each strand of hair was from its root. After a good ten minutes, the sisters completed their contribution to the artist's work. When the stepmother asked the painter what his painting meant, he replied that it reflected the fear held by people towards beautiful women in the current climate. After he presented the work to them, he packed up and left.

Back at home, Cinderella almost lost her mind when she woke up and saw the painting just as Delia was about to hang it on the wall in the main hall. She dropped to her knees and covered her mouth with both hands to stop herself from screaming. When Delia saw her reaction, she seized the opportunity to find out more from her stepsister by pretending to offer her emotional support. Delia instinctively knew that the painting must have reminded Cinderella of whatever that traumatised and spooked her. Supporting Cinderella by the elbows, Delia led Cinderella to sit on her bed. When Cinderella finally stopped shaking after almost an hour, Delia gently coaxed Cinderella to confide in her. At first, Cinderella was afraid. She felt that no one would believe her, for even she thought her story to be incredulous. When she finally decided to entrust Delia with what she had witnessed, Cinderella walked out of Delia's bedroom and pointed to the painting. She told Delia that the portrait was almost an exact representation of what she saw at the castle tower over a week ago. Delia gave Cinderella a few crayons to draw what she had seen. After half an hour of sketching, Cinderella showed Delia a near-replica of the painting. The only significant difference in Cinderella's version was that her portrait had three eyes."

Stories Travel

The situation had become untenable for Ngurunguur. His story had since been hijacked and the plot had unfolded into something beyond his control. Instead of being the director of his creation, he had to compete with not one but two narrators. Ngurunguur cannot decide if he wanted the Devil's prize more than the ability to solely steer the direction of the story. He was incensed that Twisted at first derailed his story and then simply just latched on to it and added plot and content as if they belonged to Twisted. Voice from the Heart merely stole a page from Twisted and mimicked what Twisted had done earlier. Ngurunguur must do something about such chicanery or else more would join in and he would lose his standing with the Devil. He knew that he had to eliminate his rivals' storylines in order for him to succeed in this contest. Emulating his rival's trickery, Ngurunguur picked up on Twisted's earlier story and made it his own:

"Nobody knows it but the moon possesses infinitely more power than the ability to control the tide. The souls of all living things wait for darkness to fall before they can move on to their next destination. Even if their physical selves had their existence terminated in the day, their souls can only depart when the moon appears. The sun has its role – to rot away flesh and everything the naked eye can see. The moon will then deal with the invisible spirits. Such was the natural order since time immemorial. While flesh rots away, spirits linger on and the moon has the eternal burden to decide what to do with the countless souls every second of every night. Some of them will be given another chance at living by being sent into another breathing body – a new life: a baby, a young shoot, a sapling… Some are kept in limbo, existing in their spirit form and wandering aimlessly in different planes of existence. The moon may yet assign them a physical self in due course. Waiting is the only thing left for these souls. Others may be extinguished forever. Sometimes, the moon may take in a soul for a companion.

It was in the day when Screaming Horse's soul split into innumerable parts following the destruction of the termites by the vengeful forest spirit. In that time between day and night, Screaming Horse's disassembled spirit lingered in the air above the valley of his tribe. Soon, the air cooled and the sun set. The moon crept into view when night fell. It was a bright, full moon that hanged over the valley that night. Screaming Horse's spirit waited in anticipation. Like any other night, the moon has to attend to souls all the world over. There was always time, though, to deal with every single one of them. After all, it would be several hours before the sun would reappear. The power of the moonglow will work its magic while the sun sleeps. The moon knew that Screaming Horse's disassembled soul was waiting. Still, the moon deliberately chose not to deal with it as promptly as it could. Moments before the first sliver of sunlight pierced through the horizon, the moon decided to rescue Screaming Horse and put his spirit back together. As one, his soul was gathered by the moon as she graciously made her exit. As the sun replaced the moon in the sky, Screaming Horse could be seen at the edge of the moon's sleeve as she escaped into the invisible void beyond.

The moon brought Screaming Horse back to her dwelling. There, she asked him what happened in the tent. What was in his hand when he emerged from it? What was wrapped in the blood-stained cloth? Screaming Horse did not answer. He was a warrior, not a whisperer of secrets. He did what his chief and elders told him to and he never questioned them or told anyone about his missions. It was a secret that was consciously withheld from the villagers. The moon was never one to cajole or beg. When her question went unanswered, a tall oak tree appeared in front of Screaming Horse.

Then, a tomahawk appeared. With no words spoken, the moon left. Screaming Horse stood there alone facing the oak tree and picked up the tomahawk. He looked around him and there was nothing but rocks, boulders and stony mountains. Nothing grew on the moon. Tiny rumblings were felt in the gravel he stood on. The rumblings became more violent and the ground shook. The oak tree in front of him started to move towards him. Screaming Horse could not see how that was possible. The tree had no legs. And yet the distance between him and the tree kept getting shorter and shorter. He retreated several steps and soon he started to run. Everywhere he ran to, there would be boulders, hills and mountains in his way. He swore they were not there just moments ago. But no matter where he ran to, something would appear to block his path. The oak tree closed in on him and his back would be merely a few yards from the next obstacle. Desperate, Screaming Horse charged towards the oak tree and hacked at it with his tomahawk using all his might. He had never swung his tomahawk so quickly and with such ferocity even in his most desperate battles. It would be a scene that would be repeated for the rest of eternity. Screaming Horse would succeed in chopping the oak tree, reducing it to nothing more than a stump no higher than his knee. When he finally sat down in exhaustion and relief, the oak tree would regain its original form. Once again, in front of Screaming Horse, was an oak tree that towered over him. Sick of chopping the tree that he had just reduced to a stump just a few moments earlier, Screaming Horse would get up and run. After he was tired of escaping the wooden monolith, he would face it once again and try to destroy it using his axe. It was to be Screaming Horse's fate for refusing to divulge his secret to the moon.

Kuparr imagined this story thread when he looked at another bit of his body after its disintegration. Screaming Horse gave Kuparr the chance to live a different life – the life of a courageous, stoic fighter who would be loyal and obedient till the end no matter what. Unlike the lustful, pathetic creature that he was, Screaming Horse would be his anti-thesis. Even when he was brought to the moon's abode, Screaming Horse did not succumb and maintained his dignity. Kuparr got what he wanted – a union with the moon and the end of his depraved soul. Screaming Horse's story was but a means to another end; it was the beginning of a new story thread by Ngurunguur:

'The moon that inflicted the eternal punishment on Screaming Horse had been a woman before entering the spirit realm. Her mortal experience continued to influence her behaviour as a celestial being. Contrary to popular notion, the moon was not always delicate, merciful and maternal. She could be; she could also not be. The duality in her nature stemmed from her mortal life. As a human, she lived many lives – all as women. It was in her last two incarnations that were most decisive in shaping her character as the moon. In her second last life, she swore that if she was to be reborn again, she would not just be the most beautiful woman in the world. She would be a woman of devastating beauty. She was entirely resolute in this oath that she made the ultimate blood sacrifice to ensure its fulfilment. On the night of the full moon and when Mars was also closest to the moon, she was all covered in red from head to toe and she slit her throat while muttering the incantation of Jiong. This incantation requires the person to curse everything that is sacred in their culture and their lives. They will sully and blaspheme the names of their gods, deities, ancestors and loved ones and associate them with everything vulgar, base and obscene. There were no standard lines or words to follow as the incantation was based on the cruellest of intent in the heart of the reciter. Whoever performs this ritual will get their heart's desire in the next life. Yet, it demanded a heavy price. Three, in fact. First, all existing blood relations in that present life when the incantation was invoked will die horrible deaths. There was no telling what macabre way they might die. The few in history who had used it had their relations skewered by the horns of battering rams, their stomachs cut open by the claws of rabid kangaroos, boiled alive in a well of oil by their enemies, suffocated in a gully of several thousand frogs, their eyes dug out by ravenous rats who would then enter their skulls to eat their brains… Second, the next reincarnation will be their last. After their next life, they will cease to be reborn as a mortal being. Third, in their last life, they will have nightmares every night. They will have terrible dreams of how their family and relatives from the previous life were killed. Whoever used the incantation of Jiong must have a solemn vendetta as the price to pay for it was unimaginably cruel.

The incantation of Jiong did not disappoint. While nothing could make up for her mother being torn to shreds by a troop of baboons and her father being ground to fine powder by a deranged gang of devil worshippers, the moon in her last human form was a woman of ruinous physical splendour.

She was just an ordinary looking girl before she turned fifteen. Born with mahogany brown skin, she never stood out from her peers while growing up. There was nothing to indicate her remarkable appearance later in her life that would enthral the men and haunt the women of her time. Layla was the name given to her by her father at birth. For her stunning transformation, she would also be called Gelila, Filagot, Ayana and Konjit – names that were commensurate with her wondrous outer form. The women who witnessed how the men around them became besotted with Layla were at once jealous, awed and livid. They could not understand why their menfolk fell head over heels over such a woman who was as strange as she was exceptional. Never have they seen a woman with hair of dirty mercury that shimmered in different hues of silver under the sun. It was like staring at the crude iron ores newly harvested from the mines. There was a vulgar, unminted quality to her hair, making one wonder if she had ever washed them the day they turned from unremarkable black to its silver-mercury colour. In the beginning, many doubted the authenticity of the colour of her hair. She must have dyed it, they said. That scepticism was quickly laid to rest during a storm – one of the biggest experienced in the Horn of Africa. Caught unprepared like the rest of her countryfolk, Layla (by then highly coveted by men) ran under the torrential rain as quickly as she could back to her home. Everyone saw how the first wave of rainfall caused her silver hair to erode to a dark gray and then to black. The women were smiling gleefully in the storm even as they ran for their lives. Yet, their joy quickly turned into disbelief and amazement when they saw through their rain battered eyelashes that a dull silver (the sky was dark and cloudy) crept under and through the jet black to restore Layla's crown of tungsten locks. It happened not once, but at least thrice, according to eye witnesses. Some said that an invisible witch with a paintbrush of silver must have always been flying next to Layla's head to ensure that her hair would never appear black again. Her hair was the first to change once Layla turned fifteen. A few days later, her skin took on a darker hue of brown. Slowly, over the span of a month, the colouration deepened and darkened until it was no longer possible to achieve a darker shade of brown. Then, her skin colour turned charcoal black. She did not step out of her house during this period of transformation as she was too distraught to show herself in public. Layla at that point did not understand what was happening to her. There was no way that exposure to sunlight accounted for that change. It was only the beginning. Tiny fissures started to become a feature everywhere on her skin. There was no uniformity to these cracks. Some were short, straight lines; others were in a haphazard zig-zag pattern and yet others were arc-like or elliptical. It was like looking at a parched Nile delta from above during a drought. Yet, these cracks were not numerous enough to make Layla appear disfigured. They were spaced out and instead of distracting those who looked at her, the fissures were akin to embellishments on a decorative canvas. What was even more remarkable was the light shining through these cracks. It was a dim, yellowish-white light that shone from within Layla that escaped through those breaks on her skin.

Her eyes were the next to change. Since birth, her eyes were round like grapes and she had double eyelids. Her irises were black and like everyone else, her sclera was white. With the change, the sides of her eyes elongated and they took on the shape of almonds. At the top arch of each eye was a slight indent, making out two crests on each eye instead of just one for each like everyone else. She lost her double eyelids and her irises turned white while her sclera became turquoise. It was disconcerting to look her in the eye. A pair of lights seem to be peering into one's soul, prying and judging. Her dark pupils constantly reminded onlookers that even with all the fanciful adornments and colours displayed, a highly discerning and sentient being was looking back at them. Even the most consummate of liars and the best poker-faced negotiators winced when they came face-to-face with Layla and her all-seeing white eyes dotted in the centre by the intimidating black dots that was her mind reaching out to whoever that was looking. She lost her eyebrows and her eyelashes changed from black to bright yellow.

At the end of three moon cycles, Layla's metamorphosis was complete. Standing at five foot ten, svelte and lithe like a gazelle with long limbs to match, she was a curiously wonderful physical specimen. Needless to say, she drew attention to herself wherever she went. It was impossible not to be struck by her unique features. Before she was seen as a female of marriageable age, everyone treated her with inquisitiveness and marvel. It was like meeting a new, exotic pet from a faraway land. Everyone would gaze at her hair, her eyes, her face, the pattern on her skin… And Layla let them do so without protest. Never did she feel uncomfortable with being treated like an animal on display. Once she crossed that murky threshold that separated an innocent girl from a young woman who could entertain suitors, things changed. Her peers no longer saw her as an interesting friend to have even if Layla was a constant reminder of their own physical mediocrity. Exotic, one-of-a-kind, unexplored – that was how men young and old saw her. The womenfolk were unsettled by how the new Layla had changed the game for them. Why settle for the ordinary when there is Layla the prized trophy? For thrills, men hunt lions, elephants, rhinoceros and other untamed, exotic beasts. The appearance of Layla the transformed diverted men's attention from wild game in the savannah to her. To possess her, even just for a night or a brief moment, became the obsession of any man who had laid his eyes on Layla. It drove the women mad as no man – single, committed or with wives, could deny their animalistic passion for Layla. Men refused to publicly acknowledge their lust and passion for her; yet, one look at her, or a look from her, was enough to fill their thoughts with imageries of her and the things that they could do with her.

It was wholly understandable that the womenfolk treated Layla with a combination of hidden envy and disguised repulsion. They wished their men would desire them as they would Layla. Yet, at the same time, they never stopped thinking that she might be a witch, a demon or a kind of succubus from hell sent to disrupt the lives of everyone around her. But such thoughts were kept to themselves or shared only with the closest around them. Of course, Layla knew what was simmering in every women's hearts. Another gift from invoking the incantation of Jiong was besides the recurring nightmares, Layla in her sleep could hear the innermost thoughts of anyone who had ever thought of her. No one could hide anything from her. Their faces would appear in between her nightmares and they would speak of their hidden desires. Predictably, these were mostly about men's carnal desires and women's hidden contempt and jealousy of her.

Layla used her allure over men to her advantage. Countless men would try to get close to her every day. Through them, Layla could get what she did not have. Gifts, favours, opportunities, money… anything that she wanted. Reborn in this life to a humble and honest shepherd, she repaid his love for her by getting a wealthy salt merchant enamoured with her to buy a medium-sized piece of fertile land on the river delta. With it, her father could stop his constant wandering for pasture and settle down on the land and become a farmer and still get to look after his flock. The merchant also gave him enough money to build a decent house and barns on the farm. In time, her father made a comfortable living from the fruits of the land. In her past lives, Layla never had a good and responsible father like the one she has in this present life. She repaid his goodness using her charms on men. There were several other men whom she made use of, too. She did not really bother herself with them. Yet, they flocked to her without her willing it. So, she received from them pretty dresses, earrings, bracelets, hats – adornments of all kinds. Still, she never let any of them, even the rich salt merchant, go beyond touching the tip of her fingers. That physical act was the furthest any man could achieve with Layla. None could boast of having her body as Layla was never seen meeting any of them except during the day under the watchful eye of the glaring sun in the marketplace. Every morning, Layla would stroll gracefully in the marketplace looking for things to buy for her father and his house. One by one, men would sidle up to her and start talking in mid-sentence as Layla would never lay her eyes on them or stop for them. Each had only a few minutes as another eager suitor would be only a few yards away, keeping step with them and listening to almost everything that was said. Usually, she would say something like "Yes, get me that bracelet/bangle/house and I may consider". Those men would never say no to her. Most of them wanted nothing more than a proper date with her as their first request. Only the most lascivious of them would be blatantly upfront and state that they wanted to sleep with her right from the start. Layla never responded to such shameless behaviour and continued with her business while another hopeful stud would interject with his own promises. That was how she got the salt merchant to bestow those precious gifts and favours to her father. She visited his shop often – almost every week, and he would take the opportunity to talk to her. His unsuspecting wife was never at the shop – she had to stay at home to look after their five young children, and he would flirt with her with impunity.

Like all the other men, Sarkie knew of Layla's legendary beauty ever since she matured. The first time she set foot in his shop to procure salt, he hid his lust for her by pretending to be nonchalant about her presence. He did his accounts and added up the earnings for the month while his assistant attended to Layla. All the time, he had his eye on her but he was able to disguise his gaze using his books. Only when she stepped out of his shop did

Sarkie stand up and walk towards the shop door. He stared at her back as she walked farther and farther away from him. The next time she went to his shop about a week later, he adroitly whisked his assistant away on the pretext of settling some menial task in the storage room located at the back of his shop. He began, unasked, to give a lecture to Layla on the types of salt found in his shop. Sarkie spoke of how the coarser kosher salt was preferred by discerning cooks as it was easier to pick up and spread over food compared to the finer grain table salt. He tried to impress her with stories of his travels in Palestine and beyond to India where he bought Himalayan pink salt and brought it back home to the Horn of Africa where the people saw pink salt for the first time. Just as he was about to tell her a story of his travel at sea on his way back from the west coast of India, Layla interrupted him and said that she had to be on her way.

"What would make you stay to hear my story next time?" Sarkie asked, careful not to sound too eager. After all, he still wanted to impress her with his age, maturity and experience as an older man and more importantly, as a worldly wise, successful businessman.

Layla turned her head without breaking a step as she walked towards the door. She neither smiled nor looked at him in the eye. Her eyes scanned the wooden interior of the shop from its roof to the floor and she turned her head to look at where she was going. As she walked towards the door and away from his shop, Sarkie thought that Layla's inspection of his shop was a sure sign that she would be back soon. He was eager to have her back and he would have to take greater action to lure her into his world.

Of course Layla did not go back to Sarkie's shop immediately as she was fully aware of what he had up his sleeves. That very night after she was bombarded by useless description of salt from every corner of the world, she saw him in her dreams. All his perversions were acted out in that dream. There was no mistaking his very naked intentions that involved her. She was not surprised at all. He was not the first man she met since she had blossomed to have those ideas. Layla did not return to his shop till the next month. She did it on purpose. Knowing that he was a man of resources and had sharp business acumen, she cannot make herself appear to be an easy target. Sarkie was not a hot-blooded teenage boy or young lad chasing tail chalking up experience. Getting him to give her what she wanted would require skilful manoeuvring. To cope with not getting salt every week, Layla borrowed some from her neighbours and friends. When a month was up, she made her way to Sarkie's salt shop to procure more.

Sarkie was looking forward to seeing Layla enter his shop again after that encounter. Week after week, he anticipated her arrival and was always looking at the door of his shop, hoping to catch her stepping in, her silhouette enhanced by the sun's rays. He had already prepared the stories that he would use to show off his knowledge and experience as a savvy, successful and well-travelled businessman. Sarkie imagined how she would be lapping up all the interesting details and asking him question after question. It was a hot afternoon when he was lost in his thoughts filled with images of Layla's lithe body when she finally returned after a month's absence.

This time, Sarkie was animated and effusive. He greeted Layla by waving his arms in the air and proclaimed aloud that his shop became quieter without her frequent visits. Layla, though, kept quiet most of the time and avoided eye contact. Sarkie read her behaviour as normal as they were still largely unacquainted with each other. He was determined to break the ice and get her to warm up to him. Without being asked, Sarkie launched into his pre-prepared story:

"My business brought me all over the world. Over mountains, across vast oceans and deserts – there's nowhere I've never been. I have many stories to tell you. Let me start with the most exciting one. It's on one of my many journeys across the Arabian Sea. Remember the last time you were here and I told you about the pink Himalayan salt?" Sarkie paused for a moment and took a handful of that salt from a large, tall clay pot and showed it to Layla. "It was on a sea journey from here to India that I almost lost my life. The ship was in the middle of the Arabian Sea, halfway between here and India. The sky was clear and the noon sun was shining brightly down on us. Everyone on the ship was just starting to eat their lunch on the upper deck with the full expanse of the horizon stretched out calmly before them. I was seated alone and chewing on a piece of sausage when someone shouted. Everyone looked at the ocean from portside and saw a dull, grey metallic hook on that side of the ship near the stern. At first, we thought it was the ship's anchor. But soon, another similar hook latched itself onto another part of the ship on the same side! This time, the second hook was closer to the bow. We kept turning our heads back and forth, left to right, to look at the two hooks. These couldn't be anchors for sure. One of the ship's crew, a strong, young lad in his early twenties, ran over to the first hook and tried to disengage it from the ship. In the instant that he tried to lift it off, something from the ocean darted from beneath the surface and whisked the poor fella off the ship! We gasped in alarm and all of us stood still, not knowing what to do. He was gone from the ship, that we know clearly. But why? What took him? What were the hooks for?"

Sarkie trickled the pink salt through his fingers and back into the clay pot. He moved towards Layla and beckoned her to sit on a chair in the middle of the shop. Layla sat uncomfortably at the edge of the chair and showed only her left profile to Sarkie while glancing around the shop. She took care not to face him directly to demonstrate a slight disengagement from the proceedings. Sarkie poured drinking water into two cups for them and continued:

"While we were all still reeling from the shock of the young man's unexplained and abrupt disappearance, several more hooks were thrown towards the ship and secured themselves on portside. There must have been more than ten of them this time. 'Tong, tong, tong'. I could still remember how they sound now as the metals clanged onto the ship's frame. Suddenly, we all felt a sharp thug from portside and started scrambling to grab onto something as we lost our balance. The ocean was calm. There were neither wave nor wind. Someone was using those hooks to pull the boat towards them! It must have been a group of invisible pirates using that wicked method to pull us closer to their ship and then send a raiding party to board the deck and storm the ship! Yet, in our frantic state, we could still see clearly. None of us could see where the force of the pull came from. No one dared to get close to the hooks for further examination, fearful that we might end up with the same fate as the poor crew member just moments before. Neither ship nor island were in plain sight. By now, the captain and his boatswain had rushed onto the upper deck with their cutlasses drawn. Courageously, they approached portside and took a closer look at the hooks. Before they had more than a moment's look at them, an enormous giant in the ocean must have given the hooks a big, strong pull, for everyone, including the captain and the boatswain, fell and flew violently towards portside. The ship was leaning dangerously on portside, tilted disproportionately almost to the point of capsizing. It was no easy feat to do that to the ship – it was a 100-feet baghlah, mind you! I saw some people slid off the deck and fell into the ocean. We were all desperately clinging onto whatever we could – cracks in the wooden flooring, someone's trousers, the rails on the side of the ship… anything we could grasp! What could be pulling the ship with such force? Thankfully, whatever was pulling it did not pull any harder or else the ship would have flipped over and all of us would have drowned in the ocean. Tilted that way, the ship tumbled and skipped violently over the ocean's surface for quite a while before everything stopped. We were so glad that the ship was back on even keel and everyone could sit straight and stand upright. We were all none the wiser, just glad that we were alive, save for those unfortunate few who couldn't remain on board. The captain and all his crew were at a loss as to what to do, like the rest of us. We could see the opening to a large cave that stood solitary in the middle of the ocean. It was like a mountain that arose

CHASING CINDERELLA — BROKEN DREAMS BY A.C.K. MIN

in the sea by itself. The mountain must have been at least two hundred feet high and three hundred feet across as it dwarfed the baghlah's dimensions. The hooks were still attached to the ship and we could all now see thick ropes that extended from the hooks towards and inside the opening of the cave. The ropes were made of a material no one had ever seen before. Under the light, they were almost invisible. Light shone through them and they took on the colour of the background they were held against. That was why no one could see them clearly before — they merely looked like the blue or green hues of the ocean's surface as we were being dragged across the water. Now, in the shadow of the mountain, the ropes reflected a dull, bluish grey tone. Surely, something must be behind all this! But we were also too afraid to find out what it was."

Layla stood up and made her way towards the door. She had given Sarkie enough time for today. Sarkie was taken aback by her abrupt decision to depart. He was just getting excited and had more juicy details to share with her. Layla's departure completely caught Sarkie unawares that he barely had time to stop her and call her to return. She was already out in the marketplace a few shops away before he ran to the door to catch a glimpse of her departing figure.

She did not plan to visit Sarkie's shop any time soon. Weeks passed and Layla got by with getting her salt supply from neighbours and friends. Besides, she could always get a bright-eyed young lad to fetch her some salt in exchange for a little of her time. She did not have to do much with those boys except to simply sit on a bench with one of them next to her. They would be so excited to share any bit of their lives with her and she would interrupt them by passing them a note written with the words "Get me a sack of salt". They would then rush to the shop and return straightaway only to find her gone from the bench. Naturally, they would venture to Layla's house and she would shut the door once she had the goods. The young men would be left love sick for the next few days in the hope of seeing her at the same bench again.

Worried that Layla may never patronise his shop again, Sarkie took action. He could no longer play it cool and wait it out. Regaling her with stories of his exploits was too passive. He decided to confess his feelings for her by writing her a love letter. He asked himself many times if he was foolish to do so. After all, he was already in his forties and married with children. Why would a young beauty like her see him as a romantic partner? Yet, he could not deny his desire for her. He would stare at the entrance to his shop all the time hoping for Layla's grand appearance. In the evenings just before he closed his shop, he would stand at the door and linger for a while and stare far away into the distance. And before he slept, he hoped that his wish to see her again would be fulfilled the next day. Yet, days and weeks went by and still no Layla. One day, he woke up and decided not to open his shop. He spent the whole day crafting his love letter to Layla. At the end of the day, he finally found the courage and the will to pen his thoughts to her in words. The next day, he got an errand boy to deliver the letter to Layla.

Layla always knew Sarkie would look for her. She read the letter and predictably, Sarkie spoke of how beautiful she was and how he would be filled with joy whenever he sees her. He professed undying commitment to her and wished that she could be his wife. Sarkie's heart was now at Layla's mercy and that was what she had planned for.

Although he was hopeful, Sarkie dared not predict how Layla would respond to his declaration of love. That night after he sent the letter to her, he had a fitful sleep. He tossed and turned in his bed and images of underwater trolls with barbed skin pulling the ship that he was on in the uncompleted story he was telling Layla weeks ago haunted Sarkie in his sleep. The night was still and cool. Just before dawn broke, a gust of wind from the west blew into the window of Sarkie's bedroom. Specks of gold dust that glittered with hues of orange and red flew into his left ear like an arrow. As a trader and a businessman, Sarkie had experienced many winds of change. This wind that flew into his ear though, would be the one that would change his life forever.'"

THE EPHEMERAL GYPSY

Ngurunguur paused and briefly looked around to look out for any soul that might show the slightest sign of desire to take over his latest plot. The conjuring of an exceptional and yet perplexing beauty in the person of Layla left everyone too stunned to react. While a half smile, Ngurunguur continued:

"When Sarkie woke up, he simply stared at the ceiling for the rest of the day. He waited till nightfall before he got off his bed and walked to the desert at the edge of the city. It was a good ten-mile walk from his shop but Sarkie kept a consistent pace, neither slowing down nor hurrying. He appeared to know what would await him there.

Sarkie stopped at the spot where the first grain of desert sand touched the city's outer perimeter. A gust of wind blew and he rubbed his eyes as dust and sand from the ground irritated his eyes. Blinking to get rid of them, Sarkie thought he saw an apparition slowly forming before him. Appearing just above the desert floor like a hovering spectacle was the head and limbs of someone. There was no body to speak of. Startled at seeing the entity without a torso, Sarkie took several steps back and attempted to turn around and flee. Just at that moment, an arrow flew from the top of the apparition's head – which Sarkie saw now that a tall hat was perched on top of it, and the projectile stopped menacingly just before his heart. He froze and his eyes followed the arrow as it fell straight onto the ground, only to disappear inexplicably moments before the projectile reached it. When Sarkie had recovered from his shock, he looked up but he could not find the perpetrator. He fell to his knees from fright and lay his forehead on the desert sand, his arms stretched out in front of him to assume a pose of supplication.

His body lay there – the lower half in the city and his top half (from the mid-section of his abdomen to his head) in the desert, till the next morning. An aged Bedouin with a camel stopped next to him and turned Sarkie face up. Pouring water onto Sarkie's face with his goat skin sac, the Bedouin slapped Sarkie's face a few times in his attempt to raise him. His efforts paid off as Sarkie coughed profusely and jerked his head fitfully from side to side, struggling to open his eyes while his face was still drenched.

'Son, the time for supplicating before the One has not arrived yet. The last of the last has not appeared to show the way. You are praying to a false god. He will rob you of your soul.'

Having dispensed with his advice, the Bedouin placed a tray of red dates next to Sarkie and left with the camel. Sarkie saw the man and his animal disappearing in the desert horizon under the glare of the mid-day sun. He got up and started walking, taking neither the dates nor the advice given to him by the Bedouin.

Sarkie had no clue where he was going. In the vast desert, he had no bearing except for the merciless sun that rose and set every day. He did not bother to chase the bright spot, sometimes yellow, occasionally orange and at times smeared with a tinge of crimson, as he would just be walking back and forth without progress. But the irony was that he might as well have chartered his path that way since he was wandering aimlessly in the vast expanse of sand in an extended, irregular elliptical course. For three days and nights, he trudged about lifelessly, stopping to lay himself down to rest only after the sun had set for no other reason than that there was no more light to guide his feet. Just before the sun rose after the third night, a sand storm brewed ominously in the distance. Sarkie sat up and caught a faint glimmer of light from the sun at dawn. In no time, what he made out to be a wisp of dust from beneath the horizon miles away abruptly blocked out the sun's emerging rays and suddenly sped towards him. Sarkie had no time to react and as he instinctively brought his arms up to cover his head, he felt his body being lifted by an unexplained force. As the sand storm blew about violently around him, Sarkie – even as he shut his eyes and cowered haplessly in his own pathetic embrace, felt protected and that he will be shielded from the storm and its effects. He felt as if he was placed in a cocoon and no harm will ever come to him even though he could hear the storm ravaging the protective shell he was in. He could feel himself being spun about. But compared to the storms at sea he had experienced in his travels on ships around the world, Sarkie knew that the cocoon offered a much more stable and assured shelter than even the biggest galleons made by man. He did not feel the slightest sensation of motion sickness in that mad, violent act of nature raging around him. While he felt safe, he could not ascertain when the ordeal would end and where he would be when it all ended. The unpredictability and uncertainty of the situation was worse than the imagined destruction going on around him. Sarkie only knew that he would be safe as long as he kept his eyes shut.

He cautiously opened his eyes after he felt that there were no more disturbances around him. Sarkie was afraid that the storm would return with even the tiniest gap in his eyelids. It was a risk he had to take. If not, Sarkie would be lying someplace that he did not even know for who knows how long. Nothing untoward happened as he lifted his left eyelid and saw a shimmering green expanse in front of him. Encouraged, Sarkie opened both his eyes and saw that he was at sea. Then, he realised that he felt uncomfortable, like he was lying on hard bricks. He saw that he was stretched out on a huge, gray boulder. Sarkie imagined that the boulder fell off the edge of a cliff and he was somehow placed on it and it floated in the sea with him on it. He looked around and like the desert he was in before the sand storm, there was nothing else in sight. Sarkie had gone from wandering in an ocean of sand to being lost in a desert of water.

In his travels, Sarkie had often heard of stories of men marooned, lost or bewildered. To him, these tales were all symbolic of people dealing with fear, with the unknown and with uncertainty. Now,

Sarkie himself knew very well that all three elements applied to him in his present predicament. His only salvation lay in a miracle and he closed his eyes, hoping for a genie, a sea nymph, an apparition… anything, to appear before him and offer him some kind of solution. Anything is better than him sitting alone on a floating chunk of part of a mountain in the middle of a sea that he has no name for. For hours, his wish went unanswered. Sarkie knew that this could be the end for him. He sat on an edge of that big rock and dipped both his feet in the calm sea. In all the madness that had gone on so far since he left his home, he searched for the genesis of everything. And then he realised that he had forgotten about the unattainable Layla. Sarkie looked down and stared at the waters just beneath him, where the sea swallowed his ankles, to reminiscent her beauty and shuddered to see slender, brown tentacles winding surreptitiously up his calves and working their way silently but surely towards his thighs. Before he could scamper and reach out to grip a crevice, any crevice, on the boulder, those frightening snake-like feelers tightened themselves around his legs and yanked him into the sea. Just as he was being pulled away, the back of his head hit the edge of the boulder he was sitting on and Sarkie stopped struggling with his destiny.

When Sarkie was back at home, he had turned into a completely new man. Nothing changed in his outward appearance. He remembered nothing of his ordeal in the desert and the unexplained relocation to the unknown sea. No one suspected that anything was amiss until the crafty and worldly-wise businessman started to sell off his possessions below market price. Ordinarily, no one could ever get Sarkie to shave a dime off from anything below its prevailing value. Now, Sarkie placed his house on sale and offloaded it to the first person who made an offer and it was a quarter below the price everyone deemed it to be worth. When word of the sale got around, it became the talk of the marketplace. The lucky man who bought the house could not believe his good fortune. He did not have any surplus beyond the amount he offered to Sarkie and he bid for it just to try his luck. Sarkie's house, which doubled up as his salt trading shop, had a splendid location and the buyer would be guaranteed a steady traffic to boost sales of any goods he decided to hawk.

Without his home and store, Sarkie was reduced to wandering around town like a hermit. He neither slept nor rested – everyone could see that he was walking non-stop from dusk till dawn every day; it was as if he never left the desert. Dragged from the sea by the sand-brown tentacles, Sarkie was a man possessed. The apparition that he saw in the desert – that of no torso and just limbs and a tall hat on top of a head to speak of, had targeted Sarkie for a takeover. It started the night when the ghostly gypsy blew itself into Sarkie through his ear and infected his head with the ridiculous idea to reach the desert and then wander aimlessly in it.

The gypsy never had a physical body. It was not the soul of any deceased person and had not before inhabited any living body. It came into being as a spirit and nothing else. Even so, it was incomplete. Spirits, souls, ghosts and the like have characters. Each had a mission. A vengeful spirit seeks redress of some injustice; a wandering soul looks for a refuge, either a physical body or a realm to dwell in; a playful ghost might play pranks on people. At its genesis, this entity we call the gypsy had no identity and was completely devoid of any purpose. It was part of the soul of a boy from nowhere. The boy was born in a cave within a mountain surrounded by rivers of liquid mercury and he lived there until he was almost five. He was born with the ability to walk on any liquid form and the baby unwittingly found an exit to the cave he grew up in just by haphazardly navigating the path of mercury beneath his tiny feet. At the mouth of the exit of the cave, the boy looked back into the cave and saw that he had wandered too far. But it was too late to return, for the boy was then standing precipitously at the edge of a cliff and he plunged a few hundred feet into a mud swamp below. It was at that precise moment just as the boy's feet slipped from underneath his tiny body from the cliff's rocky surface that the ephemeral gypsy came into existence. It floated there on the cliff's edge and stared at the horizon, oblivious to the calamity that just befell upon the boy who had only seconds before stood at the same spot where the gypsy now hovered over. The boy's soul lost a part of itself; the gypsy had no inkling of what it had just lost.

Without a purpose of any kind pre-defined for it, the gypsy could do anything it wanted. Besides not having any reason for being, this entity had no specific form. At the beginning of its accidental creation, the gypsy took the shape of the birds it saw nesting in the trees and flying about in the sky. After that, it decided that it would look like a worm burying itself in the mud. Insects – mosquitoes, ants, flies…, land mammals – monkeys, pigs, dogs…, sea creatures – sharks, stingrays, sea cucumbers… the gypsy had morphed into them all.

The gypsy found its powers addictive. Yet, it wanted more. Possessing varied physical forms turned into a mundane recreation to pass time. Like any sentient being, it craved for a purpose. With no one and nothing to enlighten the gypsy, it had to craft a mission for itself. If it was a caterpillar, it had to live and behave only like a caterpillar. Turning into a butterfly was amusing but it meant that gypsy had to conform to the caterpillar's pre-determined life cycle. The gypsy's power lay in its ability to be formless and still have the infinite potential to be anything it wanted to. Yet, choosing one form over another was limiting in itself.

When the gypsy flew into Sarkie's ear, it was after a decade of aimless drifting. Sometimes it stayed invisible – a formless, transparent film that floated aimlessly or merely stayed still in the air for months. Other times, it took the shape of whatever it desired. In that decade, it pondered over why it existed. Observing plants, insects, animals and people, the gypsy tried to find out what it should become so that it would have a worthy purpose. For half a year, it even turned itself into a pebble on a beach that was trampled by people and swept out into the ocean and then deposited onto another beach to be stepped on again and then taken away by the tide…

At the end of a decade, the gypsy had an epiphany: taking a physical form restricts its potential. What makes a man walk, a deer sprint and a spider spin its web? Thought is the highest form of being, the gypsy concluded. Thoughts are formless and yet they could dictate actions that have both form and consequence. And thoughts can change, can be repeated and can be erased. How wonderful, the gypsy *thought*! Even a formless entity like itself could *think*! The gypsy itself is a ghost. But it knew that it would become more than that. The gypsy will now become a thought-ghost. Without a physical body, it will inhabit not the bodies of other creatures but their minds. To make them do what it wanted them to – that will be its life's work.

When the gypsy flew into Sarkie's ear that fateful night, it was the beginning of the ephemeral gypsy's foray into the realm of thought. It would never stay in a person's head for long – moving from person to person, the gypsy's tenancy will be transient and fleeting. It would make controlling people's actions via their thoughts its primary objective, its *raison d'être*.

Controlling Sarkie was easy. His single-minded lust for Layla made him an easy object of manipulation by the gypsy. As long as Layla remains the prize, the gypsy could make Sarkie do whatever it wanted. Sarkie's wandering in the desert and being lost at sea were but thoughts planted in his mind by the thought-ghost. All the time while Sarkie was bewildered and adrift, he was lying in bed. The gypsy was merely playing tricks on Sarkie's mind. But Sarkie walking aimlessly in town and selling off his shop – those were real. The gypsy forced Sarkie to do everything that was detrimental to him just to test how far it could control a person. When Sarkie collapsed in his tattered garments outside Layla's house one evening just after sunset, the gypsy knew its work on Sarkie had reached its end. The man cannot be abused anymore. The gypsy laid him to waste (and so did Layla) and ventured to find its next victim."

The Salt Merchant's Redemption

Dead for five hundred years, the salt merchant's tale was passed down from generation to generation. Most times, it was a cautionary tale for men; other times, Sarkie's plight merely became a passing reference over coffee. 'Remember Sarkie?' 'Don't be like Sarkie!' 'You will end up like Sarkie!' Elders – grandparents, parents, older relatives, often reminded the men in their families to reign in their libido using these phrases. The poor salt merchant's legacy was a warning, a boogieman, a caricature, a joke all because of his blind lust for a beauty.

In the abyss of hell, Sarkie hid in the darkest of corners. His shame compelled him to isolate himself even as he was surrounded by sinners of the most horrendous transgressions. Sarkie was defeated by a figment of a soul. Manipulated by a whisper of a wind, he could not boast of any glorious misdeed. Humiliated for five hundred years, every passing day was but another reminder of his disgrace.

Sarkie heard every single word that Ngurunguur uttered in recounting his dishonourable life on Earth. There was nothing more ignominious than having one's own story retold by another person in one's presence. Crouched under the crevice of a boulder in a distance, every word in that story by Ngurunguur felt like an insult to Sarkie. He could feel his soul being erased bit by bit and replaced by an entity foreign to him. While alive, he had his purpose taken over by a wandering spirit that treated him as a thing to be experimented with. In death, someone deemed it fit to disregard his presence and retold his story as if it belonged to the storyteller. Upon hearing Ngurunguur's last sentence, Sarkie resolved that he would desist letting others control the storyline. While he cannot undo Ngurunguur's retelling of his life story, Sarkie could exact revenge on the gypsy by directing the course of events the way he wanted it. He emerged from beneath the huge rock he was under, climbed up and stood upon its very top. Even though Sarkie was several thousand miles from Ngurunguur, he made it a point to face the direction of the aged storyteller. Commanding attention with a voice so loud that it boomed across from where he was, every soul turned around to face away from Ngurunguur and started to listen to Sarkie's story:

"The last thing I saw as I lay outside Layla's house was of a feather floating upwards into the air. What a strange sight! A feather ascending to the sky! I did not know what it was then. Now, with the benefit of a few hundred years of hindsight, I clearly see now that it was the physical manifestation of the gypsy. Layla opened her door and stepped out to see me lying in state. I was already dead by the time she set foot outside. The feather halted its ascent in mid-air: it was the gypsy's way of fixing its attention on Layla. Crafty and shrewd as it was, the gypsy knew deep down that Layla cannot and will never be controlled by it. She was a woman of extraordinary willpower and prescience. Layla knew very well what the gypsy was even in its feathery form. They will never be adversaries or allies. The gypsy multiplied the feather over and over to form a small, compact plume, morphed into an owl and flew away. The gypsy does not know it at that time, but several months later, Layla, from another place, will watch over the gypsy's every move.

The owl flew in a northerly direction for several months. While flying over vast oceans and large tracts of land, the gypsy thought about the worthlessness of manipulating ordinary folk to do its bidding. So what if it could ruin me? There were countless salt merchants just like myself in many cities all over the world. There was no real significance in that mindless deed except to show to itself that it had the power and the ability to wreck lives through thought control. The gypsy could not find an answer to that question and continued flying aimlessly in the guise of the owl.

When it finally stopped, it was not because the owl found a purpose to speak of. It was simply bored of the skies and wanted to do something different. It landed on the top of a tall fig tree at night near an even taller castle. Not planning to do anything (it had flown about mindlessly for many months by then), the gypsy was content to stay on its perch till day break. It was a fortuitous decision because the gypsy was at the right place at dawn to witness an event that would give it its next purpose.

Not far from where it was, the gypsy heard the sound of something dropping onto the ground. It was followed by hurried footsteps that rustled the leaves and grass. Its interest aroused, the owl took flight and flew in the direction of the disturbance. It was not long before it spotted a figure running away from the castle. The gypsy's curiosity was further piqued when it realised that the person kept turning back to look at the castle tower. Surmising that it might be more fruitful to inspect the castle tower, the owl flew up to have a closer look.

By the time the owl saw the Prince, he had fully reverted to the form most who knew him were familiar with. The gypsy did not find anything amiss about the way he looked since it was the first time the gypsy saw him. Still, the owl knew that the Prince was the source of the earlier disturbance. Intrigued, the gypsy turned itself into a dark brown beetle crawling on the window ledge of the Prince's room in the tower after hovering in the sky observing the Prince.

Nothing eventful happened in the day. All the beetle could see was the Prince pacing up and down his room and whispering to himself at times. Sometimes, he would sit and think, his brows furrowed. It was obvious to the gypsy that the Prince was troubled. While the gypsy could not comprehend the Prince's actions and thoughts, it could sense that the Prince was deeply desirous. His spirit covets. More so than Sarkie, the Prince had a profound need to possess. It was as if the Prince never had anything. The Prince did not have his heart on material objects – clothes, jewels, gold… Sarkie would be satisfied when he gets Layla. The Prince, on the other hand, wanted not people, not objects, not things. He wanted the same thing as the gypsy: To become whole and fulfilled. This yearning of the Prince triggered not compassion in the gypsy but contempt. The gypsy could not bear that another entity shared the same goal as it did. From that point when the gypsy realised that about the Prince, the gypsy resolved that it would do everything in its power to stop the Prince from getting what he wanted.

The Prince had no clue what to do. He was not street smart, having been cooped up in the castle tower, surrounded by aides, tutors and royal servants most of his life. While he was conversant in the world of spells, magic and the spiritual arts, he did not know the world of men. Beyond the castle walls was a world alien to him. Where should he start looking for that servant? How would he start? What should he do? He did not have the answer to any of these questions. Seeing the Prince pace up and down the room for hours on end, the gypsy decided to take action. As a slight flutter of wind blew into the Prince's room, the beetle vanished and the gypsy flew into the Prince's head through his left ear.

The first thing that the gypsy instructed the Prince to do was to lay on his bed and sleep. The Prince did not wake up till after the sun had set. That was when the gypsy had planned for the Prince to carry out its wicked deeds. Over the course of several nights, the gypsy directed the Prince to places where royalty must never tread. What better places to bring him to than whorehouses, the gypsy thought. That would be the fastest and surest way to sully the reputation of his father and the royal household. So, night after night, the gypsy planted the devious thought in the Prince's head to revisit the women of disrepute. This went on for an entire month. But with the ushering of a new moon phase, the gypsy could not comprehend why there were not the slightest rumours about the Prince's misdemeanours. It should have become a full blown scandal by now. Was it not downright improper that he visited those houses with the loose women? There must be something that the gypsy is not getting right, it thought to itself. All this time, the gypsy resided within the Prince, in his cranium. It had forgotten that it should also observe what his victim was doing, like how it observed me in my shop, in the desert and how I stood outside the shop door looking out for Layla. That was how the gypsy knew what to do to manipulate me every step of the way. In its zeal to ruin the Prince's mission, the gypsy had neglected changing its tactics based on its observations of the target. So, the gypsy once again turned itself into the dark brown beetle that occupied an inconspicuous spot on the window ledge.

The gypsy soon realised over a week of watching the Prince that he did not venture out of his room much. That week when the gypsy did not control the Prince, he merely lay on his bed and stared at the ceiling. It was as if the Prince had lost all sense of purpose. There was no will on his part to do anything. In that time, the gypsy sensed that the Prince had started to give up on his grip on life. Having been controlled by the gypsy for a month, the Prince had forgotten who he was and what he wanted to do. There was not a time in that month when the gypsy's murmurs were not heard by the Prince. So, when the gypsy rested on the window ledge again as a bug, the Prince was bereft of a puppet master pulling his strings.

If the Prince died, the gypsy would have lost its slave. Its plan was not to kill the Prince like it did to me. That would have been too easy and it was its mistake to have ruined me so much that I died. Why not just get the Prince to jump off the tower or drown himself in the river right from the start? To control, direct and manipulate without destruction of life – that required skill. And the gypsy wanted to achieve that after his initial experiment with me.

After a week, the Prince seemed to have recovered some of his normal routine that he kept to before being taken over by the gypsy. The beetle saw that the Prince did not do much in the day. He would wake up in the mid-afternoon. Then, he would potter aimlessly around his room, occasionally picking up a book or two and browsing through them. The royal servants hardly entered his room. They would only serve the Prince when he called for them (and he did so very sparingly). Only when the moon made its appearance did the Prince become more active. He was like a nocturnal cat – listless in the day and frisky at night. The first few nights were rather ordinary to the observing bug. The Prince stood at the window ledge and propped himself up with his arms, looking out afar. The beetle could not guess what the Prince was looking for. For nights, he merely stared straight ahead, sometimes looking downwards and to the sides. The gypsy wondered if the Prince was indeed looking for something or someone, why not venture out of his tower and look for it?

To the gypsy, the week spent observing the Prince seemed liked an utter waste of time. Nothing eventful took place and the gypsy definitely did not find the answers it was searching for. Perhaps this target was not worth preying on, it thought. To the bug, the Prince was like an empty shell with no life force, purpose and meaning. The gypsy was better off looking for another person to manipulate. Just as the gypsy had that thought on the eighth night of watching the Prince, a break in the pattern occurred. At first, the change was imperceptible. The bug hid itself under the window ledge as the Prince once again stood against the ledge, looking out into the darkness. Sometimes, in order to look at the Prince, the beetle would sneak up to a corner and glance at its subject. Just a few minutes before sunrise, the bug noticed tiny strands of hair resting on the ledge, with some extending to beneath its hiding place. They slowly grew longer and longer. Its curiosity aroused, the beetle scampered to a corner to take a look. The hair on the Prince's head were all lengthening at will – some faster than others. And some of them, after extending by a few inches, started to retract. It was a puzzling sight even to the gypsy as the Prince toyed with the length of the hair on his head.

The next night, the phenomenon started earlier than the previous night. And this pattern (that of starting earlier than the night before) persisted for the next three nights. Because it started earlier and earlier, the Prince's hair grew longer and longer. By the end of the fifth night, they were so long that they extended to midway down the tower. The only thing that changed from the first night was that the Prince stopped varying the length of every single strand of hair. Now, the Prince's hair extended uniformly all the way down and only moments before day break would they return to their original state in a swoosh.

The gypsy in its coleopteron form observed the Prince for a few more nights. The Prince's hair extended all the way down to the ground at the base of the castle tower and the colour of his hair was different every single day. From jet black, it changed to purple, green, blue, pink, red… It was common for the hair colour to change a few times in a single night. In its amazement at this capricious nature of the Prince's hair, the gypsy missed out on the transformations taking place elsewhere. It was only on the twelfth night after the start of the hair lengthening phenomenon that the gypsy realised that the Prince did not look like he did in the day. At that moment when the gypsy made this breakthrough discovery, the Prince's hair was turning from ash grey to turquoise – his hair mid-way down the tower. The beetle was on the underside of the window ledge when it decided to crawl carefully back up on to the topside. With his feeble hands resting on the ledge, the Prince once again looked out afar into the night sky. The gypsy was shocked to see the visage of a young woman with full lips and a perfectly shaped aquiline nose. The eyes (one sky blue and the other gray) sparkled and shone with vigour. Any man who set eyes on this countenance would be filled with desire.

Over the nights in the week that followed, the gypsy finally comprehended why no one recognised the Prince in those places of disrepute when the gypsy controlled him like a puppet. All those times, the gypsy was completely preoccupied with directing the Prince's thoughts and actions from within the Prince that it totally neglected how the Prince looked like from without. The gypsy's objective of tarnishing the Prince's royal reputation was futile because no one saw that it was the Prince misbehaving in the bawdy beer halls surrounded by smelly drunks, the whorehouses infested with perverts, the illicit gambling dens that plundered the degenerates… The gypsy thought that it was in total control of the Prince – it could not have been more wrong. While it steered the Prince's physical actions – determining where he would go, what he would do and say, the gypsy did not realise back then that the Prince retained autonomy over how he looked. The Prince had total control over his appearance at night. This was an ability that he had forged from the countless days spent cooped up alone in his room for months and years poring over books of spells; learning, practising and perfecting the mysterious ways of mages, shamans, witches and wizards from all over the world. Not even the gypsy's thought-ghost and its wicked scheme to take over the souls of others and make them do its bidding could overcome the Prince's acquired powers.

The gypsy refused to believe that it was powerless in defining the Prince's appearance. After all, could it not just plant the thought in its subject's mind to change his looks? Finally, after so many days and nights of passive observation, the gypsy abandoned its insect form and flew into the Prince's ear just as he started to become active and looked at himself in the mirror when the moon appeared outside the window of the Prince's room in the castle tower.

In the mirror, the Prince started his nightly routine. First, he played with how his eyes looked. Every night, they would be different from the last. Yesterday, he wanted eyes that were round like pearls and he had pink irises. Tonight, he decided that he wanted eyes shaped like almonds that were longer at the sides. The colour of the irises tonight were dark like the night sky. He was in a mysterious mood. Inside the Prince's head, the gypsy saw the facial transformations taking place through his eyes. Wanting to test out its powers, the gypsy opted to change the colour of the Prince's eyes at will. But no matter how hard it tried and willed, the colour remained as the Prince wanted. The gypsy channelled all its force to focus on the colour brown as it wanted to avoid too obvious a colour change so that the Prince's suspicion would not be aroused. Never having its will rejected before, the thought-ghost encountered a crippling frustration. It almost wanted to steer the Prince to the window and make him leap through it. Controlling its anger, the gypsy started to focus on the eyes, nose, lips, ears and the shape of the Prince's face all at once. It thought that by attacking all these areas simultaneously, the Prince's ability to keep up his own looks would fail – at least one feature on his face may change according to how the gypsy wanted it. Yet, after half an hour of willing, the gypsy's shenanigans failed. Unable to understand the limitations and failings of its own powers that night, the gypsy decided to leave the Prince's head in the form of a fly. Yet, it was weakened so much by those earlier efforts that it achieved only a partial transformation – the fly had only one wing to guide it in the air. Unable to achieve proper flight, the gypsy's latest physical incarnation flew in a haphazard path and landed exhausted on the floor of the Prince's room. It was through sheer luck that it was swept under the Prince's bed by wind blowing through the same window that the gypsy had earlier planned to throw the Prince through. Under the Prince's bed, it was safe from being stomped to death by the Prince himself who was walking around the room. There, the gypsy lay for several nights debilitated by failure, frustration and exhaustion.

The gypsy could not fathom why it was unable to overcome the Prince's looks. If it could control his actions and thoughts, why was it impossible to plant the thought in the Prince's mind to change his appearance? After a week under the Prince's bed, the gypsy decided to leave the room just before the Prince woke up in the mid-afternoon as he usually did. Tired of being confined within the four walls of his room and the prison of the Prince's mind, the gypsy soared to the sky outside the Prince's tower in its earlier form of the owl. It relished the freedom of being able to do what it thought once again. Flying in the afternoon sky under the sun's reinvigorating rays relieved the gypsy of its feeling of failure to produce the changes it wanted on the Prince's face. It did not stop flying until the sun had set. When it was night, the owl perched itself on top of a tall pine tree that allowed it to observe the Prince's movements in his room.

It was a full moon that night. The gypsy was powerless as it monitored the Prince's metamorphosis. His eyes, his hair, the colour of his skin, the shape of his face, the shape of his chest, the length of his legs… As the gypsy witnessed the futility of its scheme to control and wreck the Prince's life, its bright owl eyes looked up into the night sky at the full moon. The bright, yellow surface of the full moon calmed the gypsy and made it feel better about itself. The gypsy imagined that the dark spots on the moon's surface reminded it of anything it wanted to – it could envisage out of the dark patches a map of its own kingdom where it controlled everything and dictated the wishes of all the souls there. When it felt like it, the moon also reminded it of a hapless rabbit and the gypsy would simply slice off the rabbit's ears to satisfy its sadistic impulses. The gypsy possesses a pathetic nature and it must create suffering to sustain itself.

Unexpectedly, the dark spots on the moon started to move and reorganise themselves. The gypsy could not believe its owl eyes as the spots rearranged and formed a mosaic. It was a representation of a woman's face – a face familiar to the gypsy. After staring at it for half a night, the gypsy realised that it was looking at Layla's face. It was unmistakably hers. It only had to look at her eyes – those almond-shaped, doubled crested peepers sans eyebrows, to know that it was her. That to the gypsy was the only sign it needed to know that it had to return to the Horn of Africa to look for Layla. Its work with the Prince cannot succeed until it does so. With this epiphany, the gypsy immediately took to the night sky and flew southwards."

Layla's Revenge

With a booming voice from the other side of hell, Ngurunguur was determined to wrest control of the plot back from the novice. He was not going to let another unknown wannabe storyteller hijack his idea and steal from him yet again. Since the salt merchant had the audacity to steal from the seasoned veteran, Ngurunguur merely picked up from where Sarkie left off without batting an eyelid. It was as if the story belonged to him:

"The gypsy knew that if it wanted Layla to take it seriously, it had to represent itself in human form. It cannot be a feather or an owl or anything else because Layla already knew what the gypsy was. In any case, it would be much easier to be able to speak to each other and not just rely on psychic guesswork to find out each other's motives.

Since Layla was well adept to the ways of virile men partial to her charms, the gypsy decided to take the form of a frail, old man. Appearing outside her house with a wooden walking stick fashioned from a eucalyptus tree, the gypsy knocked on the front door with the bottom tip of the stick. It was not long before Layla appeared, for she had foreseen the visit in her sleep a few nights ago. She saw the gypsy's owl flying back to the Horn of Africa from the north and peered into its absent heart. She knew full well its intentions and had already hatched a plan of her own.

Layla simply looked at the old man standing at her wooden front door for a few seconds before the gypsy realised that it did not need to begin with any preamble. It was a bizarre feeling as anyone looking into her expressionless eyes would think that Layla needed some kind of explanation for visiting her. Yet, the lack of interest in her eyes communicated focus rather than ignorance or indifference. The gypsy knew from that look that it had to come clean with its intentions or risk non-cooperation.

'You have the unique ability to see into anyone's hearts, including mine. I need your help, your power, to discover what lies in the heart of a prince living far, far away in the north. When you see him in person together with me, I want you to tell me what he is. I can control anyone's mind but yours and his. I know I can never comprehend what you are beneath your unique outer form. And I will not attempt to do so. What I want is the ability to control that prince. It is my only purpose now and I hope you can aid me,' the gypsy proposed.

'You know I have nothing to gain from helping you. If I do not state my reward for assisting you, you will be suspicious of me. You are neither man nor demon. What can I want from you? In fact, you have nothing to offer me. Do you really want my help, knowing this?' Layla replied.

Layla's question caught the gypsy by surprise. In its haste to reach her after seeing her face in the moon, it completely overlooked the transactional nature of human interaction. It was so naïve that it thought that Layla only needed its unmitigated honesty to acquiesce. Yet, at that precise moment, the gypsy had nothing to offer Layla. Standing before her in the form of an old man, it felt like a pubescent boy begging an attractive, older woman to let him have a taste of her forbidden fruits. It will never get what it wanted since it had nothing to offer in return except for its innocence. Having given the game away, the gypsy was entirely at Layla's mercy. Her refusal – a simple act for her, will be devastating to the gypsy.

'I cannot turn into a bird like you. Where you want me to go is at least a three-month journey by boat from here. If you can wait that long, I will meet you where you want me.'

The gypsy was elated. It did not expect her to agree so quickly, if at all. There was neither time nor opportunity to discuss Layla's agenda for helping the gypsy. In any case, it was not in any position to negotiate terms. After Layla told the gypsy that she would send it a sign to inform it of her arrival at Keltulop, the gypsy once again turned into an owl and flew north.

Having Layla on a long, austere sea voyage on board a barge had obvious effects on the men. Day after day, night after night, she was gawked at by the hungry hordes of unsated creatures. Yet, none of them dared to make a move on her as it would be in plain view of everyone else as Layla never seemed to leave the deck. No one ever saw her rest or sleep. She was always standing either at the bow or the stern looking out into the horizon. The simple sight of her long, red robes and silver hair being blown by the ocean winds mesmerised all at sea who looked at her. Mysteriously, she was the lone female sailing together with all the eager men. Traditional has it that having a woman at sea is bad luck. But not Layla. She was the only and constant source of joy for them even though no one dared say it out loud.

One morning just after breakfast, Layla stood atop the forecastle of the vessel and asked that all on board gather before her. She only had to whisper her wish to a boatswain before everyone scampered from wherever they were to partake in this momentous occasion. No man would miss it for the world. Everyone looked at her with a mixture of desire and awe, honoured that she had chosen them to share whatever it is she is going to say. As the first words left her lips, each of them imagined that she was speaking only to him and nobody else:

'There are the rich and there are the poor in this world. That has been the nature of this world ever since society began. Kindness in humanity has compelled the creation of the idea of giving to the poor. Yet, we know that tiny sacrifices from common folk like you and me will never be enough for all the world's poor. Does any of us here know of a beggar who gave up soliciting because he was given some money? Why don't the rich give more? If all the rich men and women in history gave up all their wealth, leaving just enough for their families and themselves to live comfortably, what would happen?'

Layla paused and took her time to look at every single man on deck. They seemed confused and uncertain. Instead of hearing from her that she required Herculean acts of masculinity to prove their worth to her, they had just listened to something that had no obvious benefit to them. Nothing to quench their thirst. No promise of 'if you do this, I will...' Undeterred, because Layla did not expect any better from them, she continued:

'This sea voyage will take at least another three months. The first man who can give an answer deemed satisfactory by me will get to follow me to my destination.'

That was not the most persuasive hook by any standard. No man would take those same words seriously if they were uttered by someone else. But from Layla's lips, that felt like a grand promise to the men's ears. The men on the barge had by then learnt about her infamous rejection of all men before them. This unprecedented dangling of a tiny piece of carrot was reason enough to get them to crack their heads on the question posed by Layla.

There was only one prize to be given to the few hundred men on the journey. And of course, no one would share such a coveted trophy with another. Who will be the first in history to have the chance to court Layla? For the entire day, no words were uttered on the ship. The only sounds heard were made by the sea, the wind and the sea birds. Every man tried hard to think of the perfect answer to Layla's question. As for Layla, for once, she was not the centre of attention. While she strolled calmly from bow to stern, from port to starboard, the men seemed trapped in a kind of daze while they rummaged their minds for the reply that will earn them the right to be her coattail.

By nightfall, one brave soul was ready. He – a short, young man with a bulging stomach who looked to be in his early 20s, walked up to Layla when she was seated on a wooden chair at the starboard, tired from standing and strolling on the deck. With his chubby cheeks, he was the last person who was expected to take the lead. Instead of a confident, charismatic pioneer, the audience on the deck waited in anticipation as this unaccomplished and mediocre buck made his attempt to wrest the reward from all who were present.

This brave first volunteer managed to impress only by being intrepid. Everything that he did – from walking up to Layla, with the wooden boards on the deck creaking indecisively, resonating the uncertainty in the quality of the answer that he had in his mind, to the downcast, reluctant look on his face as if fearful of being rebuffed by the queen, pointed to impending failure. His audience expected and predicted a disaster; by a heavenly miracle, fat boy may win the contest and that meant that they will lose and yet curiously that outcome was something that all of them were secretly hoping to witness. If nothing else, every man agreed that it was sheer entertainment.

He halted six feet from Layla and almost stuttering, the rotund young man with no name began: 'According to what you have described, no one would do anything anymore. This is because those in poverty will not do anything for a living. They would even stop begging as they now have wealth which they never had before in their lives. The rich who gave out but left enough for themselves will live in contentment, having already known and experienced a life of comfort and luxury. We will all arrive at a state where everyone is unproductive and no motivation or desire to work exists.'

Once he uttered his last word, fat boy felt like the strongest man in the world. He broke into a wide grin, puffed out his chest and looked expectantly at the only woman on the vessel. The crowd behind him was silent. Having just heard the boy's contest entry, Layla turned around and walked away from him and the crowd. As she took her first steps, she said: 'That's not good enough. It's a start, though.'

No one dared to say anything or even cast derisive looks at him as he turned around to re-join the mass of men. After all, he was courageous enough to be the first. The crowd silently acknowledged that. No one clapped as everyone was too busy digesting the implications of what just took place. The most important lesson learnt from his foray into the unknown was that there seemed to be no penalty from giving an answer that did not suit Layla's taste. The flood gates were opened. Every single man will now gun for the top prize. Desirous and covetous, they will shoot from the hip and use up every chance that they have just to gamble for the trophy. After all, they have nothing better to do and nothing to lose. What was to be a dreary months-long sea journey had now turned into an orgy of possibly useless ideas.

It did not take long before Layla regretted reacting the way that she did to the first man's answer. Before the sun set the day after Layla's first rejection, she was tired and more importantly, frustrated, from standing on the forecastle listening to the attempts of one man after another. Most of the time, as the men spoke in front of her in awe and explained eagerly to her their solutions to her age-old problem, she looked far out into the horizon or at the waves in the ocean. Sometimes, she would just glance at their faces only for a split second to amuse and remind herself how desperate and mindless men can be because of the tiniest prospect of the fulfilment of lust.

None of the answers were ingenious. All were expected. Ideas like riots breaking out, with the poor robbing and murdering the rich for the remaining wealth not given out; the rich ganging up and taking back from the poor what was given to them; an all-out war among everyone on Earth regardless of social status and background… Layla has heard them all. She anticipated all of them. The answers were as predictable as the behaviour of the men she had to put up with.

Just before the sun turned into a darker hue of orange signalling the end of the day, Layla raised her right hand high up in the air. The long queue of men before her instinctively knew that their commander had enough of listening to their proposals and quietly retreated from her. Layla had never felt so relieved. The ceaseless ranting of men was worse than the constant ogling that she had to put up with her entire adult life. She stared at the sun as it lowered itself gently and predictably into the waters. She admired its purity – strong, all-embracing and yet constant, predictable and never desirous. It gives everything that it has all the time. When it could not – due to dark clouds, rain, typhoons and storm, it was not because it refused to. Other elements simply blocked out the sun and not because it left or refused to do it work. The sun never asks for anything in return.

That night, Layla could hear and see in her dreams the answers, plans, solutions and proposals of all the men on the ship. In their excitement, the men even dreamt of what they would say to Layla the next day. Visions of utopic and dystopic futures invaded Layla's sleep. As one vision replaced another, a senseless mess ensued. Before she lay herself down on her bed, she had hoped that she could sift out among them the one who could provide the answer that would satisfy her. But in the melee that night, it was impossible to even make out a single, coherent narrative that was remotely logical.

The next day after the morning meal, Layla sorted out the men who had already given their answers from the rest. From then on, everyone who had a chance to present their ideas to Layla will be confined to their bunks. They can only emerge at night when others had retired. They will spend the entire night awake on deck. Layla devised this plan to reduce the number of men who would be sleeping at night so that she can dramatically increase her chances of identifying the one person who might have an answer that was sensible enough for her to declare it to be the winning one. After all, each man was never told that they could only have one idea. If Layla did not separate those who already have their chance from those who have not, she would be facing a nightmare horde of useless dreams every night. She was not willing to put up with this outcome. If the right answer came along in the day, then of course the work for her was done.

As expected, no man satisfied Layla on the second day. That night, even though about a quarter of them were on deck, Layla still could not sieve through the cacophony of voices in her head to locate the right man with the right answer. This went on for another two days. With half the men on deck at night on the third night of the contest, Layla thought that she might just have a glimpse of a promising dream by one of them. Yet, she was to be disappointed. But this time, the negativity extended to herself. She woke up and felt disgusted as she realised that it was she who was now desirous. Layla felt ashamed that of all the people on the ship, she wanted more than the men. Each man had wanted only her. Now, in her quest to find out who possessed the answer to her question, she wanted every man on board – if only what were on their minds. In principle, she was much, much worse than them. Indignant and proud, she could not admit it to them. Layla had to see the contest through if only to preserve her reputation. Only by continuing this charade will the men remain oblivious to Layla's flaw.

At the end of seven days, Layla had gone through all the men on board, save for one. He was not exactly a man. Like Layla, he was unique on the baghlah as he was the only boy while the rest of the males were adults. Yet to hit puberty, he was only eight years old. He was on a sea voyage with his grandfather who, despite being all of eighty, still found himself wanting to take part in Layla's contest with his feeble, old man story. Just after noon on the seventh day of the contest, for the first time in a week, there was no longer a queue before Layla. Having heard the effort of the final person, Layla was perturbed by the notion that she was not able to suss out even a single idea worthy of her approval despite all her efforts in the day and at night. It was at this point, when Layla was most disheartened, that the boy's grandfather walked the boy up to her. He told Layla that she had to hear his answer. 'Because it is brilliant in its simplicity,' he said. Layla looked at the boy and asked for his name. 'Chibuzo,' came the reply.

'So, Chibuzo, let me hear if your answer lives up to your grandfather's acclaim,' Layla spoke in a calm voice that masked her exhaustion and dispiritedness.

In his pre-pubescent, high-pitched tone typical of boys his age, Chibuzo began: 'Madam, I will tell you my conclusion before boring you with the details: If every wealthy person in the world did what you have suggested, nothing will change. After receiving money from the rich, the poor will spend them all in no time. And they will revert to their former poverty-stricken status very quickly. But the rich will increase their wealth because they got to be rich by knowing how to make money and make their money work for them. The world will not change, hence. So, Madam, are you happy with my answer?'

Her eyes lit up. Chibuzo's solution to her question lacked all the pretentious and unnecessary complications conjured up by all the men before him in their attempts to impress her. Still, Layla did not want to be seen as being too lenient and going easy on a young boy just because of his age. He had to prove his worth in front of the horde of hot-blooded men looking at him now – men who embodied the vices and virtues that he will one day possess, too. Besides, Layla wanted to test if the boy had the right substance to back up his promising thesis.

'Do continue with the details like you promised,' she replied matter-of-factly.

Without so much as a word, Chibuzo took a small step forward and stretched out both his arms to take Layla's left wrist gently. All the men gasped at the young boy's audacity to lay hands on the coveted prize of mankind. Layla did not react and the absence of any resistance by this powerful woman was enough to convince everyone on board that they should not dictate what was appropriate in that circumstance. Chibuzo proceeded to place Layla's left hand on top of his head and he rested her hand on his head for what appeared to all observers to be only a few seconds. What transpired in Layla's head, though, was very different. It felt like an eternity to her.

Right in front of Layla, above the ocean and in the sky before her, armies of men, of beasts, of mythical creatures – fairies, gnomes, elves, trolls, golems, griffins, unicorns, cyclops, garudas, Oriental dragons, enenras, rikshas, crocotta... appeared. There were so many of them that she could not immediately recognise every single one of them. The beasts and mythical creatures were all in their natural forms. The men, though, kept changing. They first appeared as primitive, unarmed cavemen from the prehistoric era. Then, the cavemen turned into warriors with weaponry and armour. Some resembled the Viking berserkers, some looked like the Japanese samurai, others had similarities with the Aztec jaguar warriors, Sioux braves, Bugis fighters, Maasai warriors... Later, their fighting gear evolved and became more advanced and sophisticated. The men would eventually use weapons and equipment that Layla could not recognise. Projectiles that were infinitely more lethal and potent than the bows and arrows used by the horse-riding Mongols. Steel birds controlled and steered by men that were seemingly indestructible and rained hell everywhere below with their droppings. Entire cities were obliterated in seconds in explosions that culminated in large mushroom-like clouds. Right at the end, Layla saw that the world she lived in – the one presently with everyone she loved and hated, vanish without a trace, emitting light in all directions before it was extinguished. Throughout the entire vision before her, there were no interaction between and among the men, the various beasts and the huge array of mythical creatures. They merely existed as an evolving, shape-shifting mural albeit on an astronomical scale.

After what seemed like less than ten seconds, Chibuzo freed Layla physically and mentally and Layla fell to her knees. Thoroughly exhausted from witnessing the brutal and tragic span of history and a future that she will not live to experience, tears rolled down her cheeks. Even though she felt immense pain and sadness, she was grateful to Chibuzo for the tragic revelation. The vision that Chibuzo imparted to her made Layla realise that her question of wealth versus poverty was an important but ultimately narrow one. More importantly, her focus on it was meaningless. Chibuzo showed her that nothing will change the inequality that had existed and it will persist. Regardless, all will end in death, despair and nothingness.

The men on board were speechless at the fall of the Layla the haughty. It was implausible that the queen of their hearts, so cool and measured, could be made to reveal her vulnerabilities by a scrawny young boy. With the contest over, Layla no longer appeared on deck in the day. She spent daylight in her private bunk sleeping, waking up only after sunset to look for Chibuzo after eating at night her only meal of the entire day. Chibuzo became the envy of every man on the vessel for he alone could be beside Layla every single night. Layla summoned Chibuzo not just because he won her contest. It was his innocence and purity that she admired. She theorised that she was unable to detect Chibuzo's thoughts in her sleep because he never thought about her. While every hot-blooded man on the ship had Layla on their minds all the time, Chibuzo was hardly ever pre-occupied with her. He thought about her question and not her. Even so, her question merely took up a few minutes (or even less) of his time.

Layla wanted to find out more about what Chibuzo knew. While she could peer into the hearts and minds of men, her abilities did not extend to the universe. What secrets lay within Chibuzo's mind? The fate of humanity, of the world, of the stars beyond, the universe... The world of men had already begun to bore her long ago. It became predictable and uninspiring after Layla spotted the patterns of lust, desire, conceit, greed, envy, anger... repeating and recurring infinitely. She needed Chibuzo to deepen her enlightenment.

The first night Chibuzo was on the deck with Layla, Layla took his hand and led him to portside while the ship sailed silently under an overcast sky. It was the start of a new moon cycle and the waxing crescent moon could barely be seen behind the clouds. They stood admiring the serene calm of the night sky lightly illuminated by the new moon. Layla knew that Chibuzo was the right person to edify her because without any words exchanged between them, mythical dragons appeared high up in the night sky. No one else except Layla and Chibuzo could see them. While the rest on deck only saw what they could not have, Layla and Chibuzo witnessed dragons from forgotten lores soaring and hovering in the sky above them. It was an amazing sight for Layla. She had only heard about these remarkable creatures from tales spread by travellers and storytellers who spun fantastical plots that revolved around them. Never in her many lives did she ever thought that it was possible for her to see them in front of her in all their magnificent glory. An entire flock of fire-breathing dragons, armed with talons that looked infinitely more menacing than the Claymores wielded by Scottish highlanders, with wings that covered several feet – wider than the roof of her house, and eyes that sparked fear and awe in all who looked into them, filled the night sky. Remarkably, despite their terrifying reputation and fearsome appearances, Layla never felt so calm looking at these now extinct beasts in their element. They did not bother Layla or Chibuzo and appeared to be relishing their lost moments in space and time if only because of the magic of the young boy with immaculate thoughts. Layla never felt so liberated, having been the sole focus of attention all the time when she was among people. That night, she was free to be herself and she directed all her attention onto the chimerical beings that did not care for any person in their primeval realm where they ruled eons ago.

For the next two nights, Layla looked for Chibuzo to relive the magic of their first night together on deck. Chibuzo was never one to initiate contact. He was contented to be in the care and company of his aged grandfather who seemed much more eager than him to announce Layla's arrival every night. It seemed out of turn that the unattainable and haughty woman so admired and desired by many would be actively requisitioning the companionship of underaged Chibuzo. To the lascivious observers, they could not fathom the platonic, immaculate interaction between Layla and Chibuzo. All they witnessed were two people standing on deck the whole night looking at the emptiness of the night sky above and beyond them. To them, those nights were extravagant, mindless loss of opportunities.

Layla's pleasure would not last endlessly, for Chibuzo had a story to reveal to her. On the fourth night of her bliss on deck under the stars with the pubescent boy, the dragons were again brought out to play by Chibuzo. All these nights, no one could see Layla's bright and guileless smile at the state of nature above her because the observers stood a respectful distance away from them in the dark. Besides, her face was always turned away from them and tilted up towards the night sky. That night, Chibuzo allowed the wondrous creatures to frolic in the heavens for an hour. Then, one by one, the flying leviathans disappeared from sight. Layla became more and more frantic once she realised what was happening. The night sky looked barren and desolate without their fiery eyes and raging balls of fire that spewed from their mouths. She turned to Chibuzo on her right and pleaded with her eyes. Layla knew that this was Chibuzo's doing. Chibuzo looked back at her, revealing no emotion, except having the look in his eyes similar to that when a young child wanted others to know that he had already tried his best. That was when Layla realised that Chibuzo was trying to protect her from the truth. That night, she was not sure if she was ready to see what Chibuzo was protecting her from. It was still a good few hours before dawn would break when she looked up for the last time that night and saw a wingless, snake-like dragon with bright yellow scales sporting horns and whiskers on its visage. It was the only dragon left. For the first time, Layla retreated into her private cabin before the sun rose. The men on deck parted to form a make-shift corridor made up of their bodies to allow Layla to pass through. Even though they were thrilled to come into contact with her flowing robes as she walked past them, they could not avoid sharing a tinge of the deep sense of gloom and dread felt by Layla. After Layla had gone out of their sight, the men shuffled quietly back to their cabins, disappointed that their viewing of her was cut short that night. They were also perturbed as to why Layla was no longer as exuberant as before after spending the night with the boy.

Layla would not emerge from her cabin for a few more nights. This unusual phenomenon became a cause of anxiety and consternation among everyone on board except Chibuzo. By the third night of her absence, a riot almost broke out. The men could not stand not being able to see her any more. Some of them blamed Chibuzo for this development and threatened to harm the boy. To protect his charge, Chibuzo's grandfather made his way to Layla's cabin and pleaded with her to show herself, even if it was just to take a short stroll on deck. Layla knew that Chibuzo was not to be blamed in any way for her behaviour. She knew that she had to be grateful to him for those feelings of elation and joy during those magical moments that he had conjured for her. That night, Chibuzo was merely going to show her the truth which she was not prepared to face. To allow the men to harm Chibuzo due to their sheer ignorance would be most unacceptable.

Layla emerged from her cabin to forestall any worsening of the situation. As usual, her appearance compelled the men to be on their best behaviour. Any talk of violence and harm to Chibuzo was immediately silenced as she went onto the deck and made her way to the forecastle with quiet, stately dignity befitting of royalty. The men followed her like a pack of lionesses would a lion. Without a word, Chibuzo's grandfather ushered his grandson to where Layla was, for the aged man knew what was at stake. Chibuzo took a good, long look at Layla, as if he was the one with more experience and knowledge, and Layla smiled. With that, she gave her unspoken consent for Chibuzo to begin at that moment what Layla refused to witness a few nights ago. Dragons started to appear in the night sky. Ten, fifty, a hundred, thousands... Layla withheld any feeling of joy for she understood that it was not the beginning that will be important that night. True enough, after about ten minutes, the number of creatures in flight started to decrease. Slowly but surely, Layla could tell that there were fewer and fewer of those delightful, noble beings. When she spotted the same wingless, yellow serpentine dragon from a few nights ago soaring across the moon, Layla braced herself for what Chibuzo had for her.

There were no clouds that night. Layla could see clearly that an elongated object was emerging from the quarter moon. As more of the object presented itself, she realised that she was looking at the bow of a wooden boat. It was a small vessel that resembled a Polynesian war canoe. She could see that there were several men on board the *waka taua*. From where she was, it looked as if the boat and the men were like shadow puppets as she could not make out the finer features on their faces and the hull of the canoe. Also, it was not entirely clear if they came out of the moon or they appeared from behind it. Regardless, once that first *waka taua* appeared completely in the night sky, more and more canoes and men appeared. The small naval war party that was airborne soon began their pursuit of the horned dragon with whiskers. They zigzagged across the vast expanse of the sky as the dragon meandered and twisted its long, sinewy body around, under and over invisible obstacles.

Layla now understood what happened to the other dragons. They did not vanish randomly. Through this last wingless dragon, Chibuzo wanted to show Layla the fate that befell the entire species. There were supposed to be several thousand more of the war canoes. Chibuzo was compassionate enough to avoid showing Layla a bloody spectacle across the night sky. He could have painted the entire night sky red with the blood of all the dragons. One, though, was enough for him to make his point.

The men on the canoes have resorted to standing on their boats and throwing spears at it. A few of those projectiles have skimmed off its hide; none have yet penetrated any part of its body to inflict any real injury. Layla could tell that this last dragon was tired and frustrated from having to evade its pursuers. It kept trying to seek refuge near the moon, pausing for a few moments every now and then, surveying its attackers and the direction of their attacks and then taking flight again. None of its attackers have given up and they have yet to exhibit any sign of slowing down; Layla knew it was a matter of time before one of the spears would finally find its target and the dragon would fall prey and succumb to more and more injuries. Before the inevitable conclusion, Layla turned and looked at Chibuzo. She placed her right hand on his left shoulder and a tear rolled down her cheek. The moonlight reflected off Layla's still stoic face an appeal which only Chibuzo could fathom. Having experienced neither ecstasy nor despair in his short, young life, the boy was nevertheless equipped with the uncanny ability to be prescient of the desires of others. His grandfather said this was a gift from the gods to his grandson to make up for the loss of his parents at birth. Chibuzo never had the chance to utter their names in their presence. No one even knew where their final resting place was. In response to Layla's plea, Chibuzo squat down and placed his left hand under Layla's right foot. He lifted her up with that single hand and stood up. Just as that happened, a thick fog enveloped the entire barge. Chibuzo's grandfather could not even see his own fingers when he stretched his arms out to balance himself during the ensuing confusion on board.

While everyone else on the vessel were preoccupied with not falling overboard, Layla was trying to find her feet in the air. It was an amazing feeling to be able to walk upwards, downwards, laterally, diagonally up and down, in ascending and descending spirals, literally in any conceivable direction, in mid-air. Chibuzo was not with her. He was still on deck and Layla could see that he was the only person on the barge who was not surrounded by the fog. She understood that he lifted her up into the sky for a reason and she went to work immediately. Gingerly, she moved her feet and tried to make her way in the sky. Stepping on air, on nothingness, was nerve wrecking. She wished that there were more clouds in the sky that night. They could have acted as stairs for her to step on and she could even have rested her arms on them for balance. She tried to imagine tiny little wooden steps where she was going to place her feet and took a few small steps. Slowly, Layla gained more confidence and moved a few inches from where she first was. As she became more assured of her technique, she found that she could in fact glide instead of walk. Since nothing defined how a person should move in mid-air, she started to skim on nothingness one foot at a time. This way, imaginary wooden steps were no longer needed as Layla dictated where she wanted to head to just by looking at the direction of her travel and she will glide to her destination. It was almost as if she willed her way effortlessly once she mastered the technique.

While Layla experimented, the situation for the lone dragon had gotten more desperate and dire. The men from the war canoe were able to inflict more injuries to it with their projectile weapons which also included stones hurled from slingshots. The dragon showed signs of slowing down and it also needed more rest from time to time compared to before. Layla knew that she had to get to it urgently to prevent the inevitable conclusion from arising. She ascended higher and higher into the sky by imagining that she was ascending a spiral staircase and glided upwards in a zig-zag fashion, ignoring that there could be steps to negotiate. This way, Layla achieved a rapid rate of ascent even though she felt dizzy from having to rise upwards so quickly in an imaginary vertical column. Once she got onto the same horizontal plane as the dragon and its pursuers, Layla had to be skilful to avoid being caught in the chase. Avoiding spears, stones and other projectiles, Layla made her way closer to the dragon. She was more agile and could manoeuvre quicker than the men with their canoes as she was tiny and unencumbered by the long wooden hulls of the *waka taua*. The dragon also seemed to be unaware of her presence given that its soon-to-be killers were visibly larger and more menacing. Like a fly, inconspicuous and yet full of intent, Layla managed to avoid detection and succeeded in going so close to the dragon that she could grab its tail.

The dragon at first did not feel Layla's grip on the end of its tail. Its senses were too preoccupied with evasion and flight that her tiny hands (in relation to the gigantic creature) did not invoke any sensation. While it was taking a short breather from its pursuers, it could feel something pulling on its tail. Frightened, it jerked violently and thought of fleeing again. As the dragon coiled and turned its head to look at its rear end, it was shocked to see a woman holding onto its tail for dear life. She seemed incapable of harming it and in fact, the dragon thought of protecting her from the men even though it was unable to guarantee its own safety for the past few hours. Knowing that it does not have much time to spare, the dragon curled itself up into a ball so that Layla could reach one of its long, thick whiskers. She grabbed one of the dragon's whiskers and using it, climbed onto the dragon's large, bulbous nose. Sitting on the dragon's nose, Layla stared into its eyes and said aloud that it has to fly into the moon to escape its attackers. She did so not knowing if the dragon could understand any of her words. But she could not have done it using any other way and time was not on their side.

Miraculously, the dragon understood her perfectly. Looking up to its left, it saw that the moon was not that far away. The nearest war canoe was perhaps just under a nautical mile away. It would take just a few seconds for it to reach the moon. It was tired from being chased all over the heavens the entire night and Layla's solution was better than what it had done so far. Without any hesitation, it mustered all the remaining strength in its embattered body and made a final, desperate lunge towards the shiny crescent high up in the sky. It flew towards it like a javelin – hell-bent towards its target without any thought or consideration for its safety, for after all death at the hands of the men on the *waka taua* was the only other option. Layla was unable to remain seated on the dragon's nose, however large it was, due to the terrifying speed. Just as the dragon was going to enter the moon's atmosphere, she fell off its nose but she was able to hang on to one of its long whiskers with both hands just for a brief moment. Before she loosened her grip, she shouted: 'Turn into a snow rabbit once you are on the moon. Those men won't recognise you that way!' As she slipped and tumbled away in the darkness of space, the dragon disappeared into the dark side of the moon. As the morning sun slowly crept back into the sky to regain its place, Layla caught a glimpse of the last segment of the dragon's tail before she lost sight of it.

Chibuzo saved Layla the effort of having to make her way back to the barge. He willed her back onto the vessel and cleared the fog. By that time, dawn had broken and the men were exhausted and confused from wandering around aimlessly on deck the whole night. As they retreated to their cabins to rest, Chibuzo looked up at Layla and said:

'You don't owe me anything. No one else could have done that except you because you, unlike others, loved them and saw the good in them whereas others saw harm and felt fear.'

After that night, Layla never looked for Chibuzo again. She spent the rest of the journey in her cabin. Night after night, the men lined up along the narrow corridor outside her cabin to await her grand appearance. But they waited in vain day after day, night after night. Some were even reluctant to get off the barge when the vessel reached their port of call. They longed to see Layla for one last time before they disembarked. Yet, it was not up to them to decide if their out-of-sorts maiden would emerge. She finally emerged one day. But that was simply because the barge had arrived at the nearest port to Keltulop. After slightly over three months, Layla had completed her sea journey and she was ready to meet the gypsy as planned. She did not look for Chibuzo to bid him farewell when she got off the barge. She knew that sometime in the not-too-distant future, she would have another chance to thank him again.

Layla paid for a horse and rode to Keltulop. It would take her two days and one night to reach the city. After riding for a day, she checked into an inn. It was a full moon night. She had not looked up to the night sky since that eventful night in the heavens with the wingless dragon. Looking at the bright, full-faced orb, she was grateful once again to Chibuzo as she could clearly see the ears of a rabbit. 'It must be the dragon. It is now safe from its attackers since they could not see that it has since transformed into a snow rabbit in the moon,' Layla thought to herself. That night, she slept soundly knowing that the last of dragonkind was safe in the refuge of the moon.

The next morning, Layla continued her journey to Keltulop. Just as dusk fell, she arrived at the city gates and saw the moon rising slowly up into the heavens again. It seemed larger and rounder than the previous night and also appeared much closer to her than ever. She stretched out her arms and felt that she could almost touch the moon with her hands. 'I must be dreaming,' Layla thought. She brought the moon close to her face and kissed it. Just before she released it back to where it was previously, Layla whispered to the moon: 'Summon the gypsy to me.'

At the far side of the other end of Keltulop, the gypsy was hiding in a crevice in the trunk of an oak tree in the form of a green tree snake. It was tired of waiting for Layla for months on end and decided to laze the days away uneventfully as an inconspicuous reptile. At precisely the same moment that Layla sent for the gypsy, a tiny white rabbit stuck its little head into the crevice of the oak tree where the scaly gypsy lay. Intrigued and challenged by the audacity of that creature, the snake sprang into action. However, the rabbit was much more alert and agile than the snake had expected it to be. The rabbit leapt away and was already several yards ahead of the snake by the time the serpent had crawled out of the tree and onto the forest floor. As the gypsy gave chase, it saw clearly that it was losing more and more ground with every second that passed. To catch up, it first turned into a brown hare. It leapt and bounded furiously across the forest floor in pursuit of its target. Yet, despite its powerful hind legs, the gypsy in its new form could not bridge the by now seemingly huge distance between it and the elusive rabbit. It resorted to morphing into a greyhound and still the speed champion of canines could only do so much to cut the gap. Frustrated, it decided that a racehorse, ripped from neck to tail purely with muscles designed solely for a single purpose, would be the best candidate to catch up with the rabbit. It was right. Within a minute, the horse came close to trampling on the tail of its prey. Just before that could happen, the gypsy once again changed into a snake – this time a Burmese python, and launched itself ruthlessly like a spiralling arrow through the air with the aim of coiling its sinewy body around the elusive rabbit to immobilise it for good. But the rabbit was too quick for that tactic. It sprung high up into the air the moment the horse transformed into the reptile. In its latest form as a peregrine falcon, Layla's messenger soared into the night sky. As the Burmese python crashed onto the ground, it realised it was chasing something as sneaky and capricious as itself. No longer was this just about matching its prey's speed. The gypsy has to catch up or be faster than its prey to assuage and repair its damaged ego. Rising from the ground, the gypsy chose the form of a phoenix for this crucial mission. With a demonic look in its eyes, the phoenix went after the falcon brimming with absolute confidence that it would soon be beak to beak with it for the phoenix to grab it with its claws and then tear it apart. The vertical climb of the phoenix was impressive. It was almost halfway up in the sky in a matter of seconds. Its cockiness, though, also lasted only that long, for it soon found out that it was flying after a mirage. What it thought to be the falcon's tail was nothing more than moonlight itself. From the crevice in the tree, to the forest floor, to the night sky, the moon made the gypsy go where it wanted to. The phoenix was never going to reach the moon no matter how skilful it was in the air. After spending almost an hour in futility, it decided to let nature do its work and it descended slowly to the nearest tree top. Exhausted, it perched on a pine tree but even so, it refused to take its eyes off the moon. Staring angrily at the shiny orb in the sky, it took the gypsy quite a bit of time to comprehend the purpose behind the chase. When it finally realised that Layla was behind the rabbit's trickery the entire night, the gypsy was aghast at its stupidity.

Knowing very well that Layla would always be several steps ahead of it, the gypsy decided to bide its time. The light cast by the moon that night had a life of its own. Following a path dictated by a power known neither to nature nor the gypsy, the moon beam took its time to reveal its true path. Sometimes, it moved across the ground rapidly, seemingly taking a logical, well-trodden path down a road frequented by travellers; other times, it traversed the earth randomly in a haphazard fashion in no discernible pattern. To amuse itself pending Layla's final sign, the gypsy changed to a gryphon, a gamayun and then a garuda. Finally, a phenomenon occurred that the gypsy, even in its boredom, could not ignore. The moon disappeared without any warning (it was a cloudless night) and all sources of light were extinguished. It did not last long – the garuda's heart beat a total of three times in that brief interregnum. But it was the signal that the gypsy was waiting for that night. In that time of absolute darkness, a deep red glow emanated from a hut to the south of the pine tree. As soon as the sky and Earth were restored to their original state of being, the garuda flew south in response to Layla's command.

Layla was sitting on a cheap stool in the hut awaiting the gypsy's arrival. In front of her was a nondescript table fashioned out of birch. A lit red candle and a dome-shaped bird cage rested on top of it. The windows were opened and as the wind blew through the hut, a single feather of golden yellow hue wafted into the hut. Layla opened the tiny door of the cage and patiently waited for the feather to slowly and gently settle into it. Once it entered the cage, she closed the door and a yellow-breasted robin materialised and the feather was no more. Layla blew the candle out and retired for the night.

The next morning, the yellow-breasted robin sat in the cage patiently and respectfully. By choosing to be a small bird that fit in the modestly sized cage, the gypsy was showing Layla that it was going to listen to her wishes. Seeing that, Layla opened the door of the cage and released its willing captive into the open. Once it flew out of its confines, the gypsy transformed into a young man and stood beside the birch table and awaited Layla's instructions."

The Trap

"It did not bother the Prince much when it happened the first few times. He thought he must have been either too tired or tipsy to accurately ascertain what he saw. Then one night, he saw that face again – this time it was in a dream. It looked exactly like himself when he was debauching and debasing himself in the houses of ill repute around town at night. He was looking at a woman looking back at him as if he was staring at a mirror – those seductive eyes with the different coloured pupils looked right straight into his own. The only oddity was in that dream, those eyes seemed to communicate silently but clearly to him that she knew him – not just his name but his origins. It shocked the Prince in his sleep to realise that someone out there might know his secrets. He woke up with a start and sat upright in his bed (it was almost dawn) and thought hard about it. The Prince started to recall that perhaps a few weeks ago, in one of his nocturnal gallivanting jaunts around town, he saw from the corner of his eyes a woman of unusual and striking appearance standing alone near a table in a bar frequented by passing merchants. He did not pay too much attention to her as he was too pre-occupied with fending off the unwanted (yet strangely much appreciated) attention of a drunk. The Prince tried to recover in his memory any other time when he might have seen someone like her from that night onwards. As he sat there alone in the darkness, he could slowly but surely recall more instances of the stranger's sightings. He recalled at least two other occasions when a woman with a similar appearance stood some distance away from him. He could not fully explain to himself why he had not paid more attention to her then. There was no good reason to anyway since their paths did not cross even though they were at the same place at the same time.

That night, the Prince decided to go about his nightly activities as usual. Yes, the dream bothered him. But it was not enough to deter him from performing his nightly duties. Transformed, he decided to pay a visit to a notorious gambling house known for being very selective with its clientele. Not anyone can enter the premises – its owner, a levitating dwarf with no limbs, called the shots and scrutinised everyone from top to toe before granting permission for entry. The Prince in his womanly form never had any problem with gaining entry as the dwarf knew that more men would flock to the den and part ways with their hard-earned money every time she was in the house.

There was an unusual game at this particular gamblers' hideout that cannot be found elsewhere. The usual games of bridge, blackjack and poker were the staple here like in other gambling houses. However, this den operated by the bizarre looking dwarf offered a unique proposition. And it would take a person of enormous courage (some say stupidity) to partake in it. Called 'Pinky Winky', punters placed their bets on a group of people (it takes at least two to play) who would stare at each other; they can try their luck in choosing who will blink first, second, third, etc. This was a high-stakes staring contest for those in the game and not the bettors. Whoever blinks first will have one of their pinkies cut off. If the loser has no more pinky left to slice (from the sheer foolishness of playing again after having lost once), the other fingers will have to go. First to be cut after the pinkies were gone would be the ring finger, the index finger, the thumb and then the middle finger. The middle finger was the last to be chopped off because it served as a symbol of defiance for the idiot who did not know when to quit; it was the only semblance of dignity left that was given to the ultimate loser. Talking about the greatest loser of all, the current owner of this gambling house was its greatest personification: the limbless dwarf was given the ownership of the joint after he sportingly played and lost all his fingers and then his limbs. His legs were the last to go. He made the request to chop off his hands before his legs as he said that he could at least flee his debtors if he wanted to. The previous owner of the gambling den – a 500-year-old magi, was so impressed by the dwarf's simplicity and daring honesty that he gave the limbless man the gift of levitation together with the title deed of the property before leaving. The magi was never to be seen or heard from again. Since then, no one has ever lost more than a finger playing Pinky Winky.

All eyes were on the Prince (or should we say Princess) as he entered the room. Tonight, he had long, wavy hair in bright fuchsia. The Prince looked practically naked from the rear as he wore a white strapless satin dress that exposed the entire back. The men of Keltulop have been wondering night after night the identities of strange, stunningly beautiful women who kept appearing in different parts of the town after dark. Yet, no one could achieve any intimate knowledge of these beautiful creatures. The appearance of the Prince in his titillating outfit made each and every man in the room think that they might just be the lucky one that night. The attention of everyone in the room would have continued to be fixated on the Prince if not for someone shouting 'Pinky Winky' at the top of his voice. It was an ordinary looking young man dressed in a farmer's overall. The rule of the house was that the game must be played whenever someone shouted its name. And the first person who was touched by the one who called out Pinky Winky would have to play the game with the initiator. Tonight, the young man walked calmly to the Prince and gently tapped her on her bare right shoulder. Everyone gasped at the prospect of the desirable woman of unknown origins squaring up against the daring young chap.

The dwarf looked at the young man and the feminine Prince and then glanced knowingly at a wooden square top table located at a corner of the gambling den. They did not need a second invitation and the two of them moved across the room and sat opposite each other. More eyes were on the more desirable of the two, naturally. No words were needed at all. Everyone knew the rules of the game – the first who winks, loses and then out comes the knife and the chopping board. The levitating dwarf hovered between the two contestants, positioning himself so that the two cannot look at each other eye-to-eye before the start of the game. He stayed between them long enough for everyone to place their bets. Once the house was ready, the dwarf gravitated upwards just above their foreheads and shouted 'Stare!' That's when the fun starts and everyone was hushed; all eyes will be moving back and forth between the competitors to detect the slightest sign of weakness in the two rivals.

The odds seemed to be stacked against the young man. The Prince, expressionless, proud and unattainable, seemed like a safe bet for most in the house. His aloofness reminded most of the men present of the females they had encountered throughout their lives who gave them blank stares and disinterested glances when they were trying to get their attention. The young man, perceived by many to be merely a young buck trying to punch above his weight, was doomed, they thought. He will learn his lesson, the men whispered among themselves. Nothing happened for a full five minutes, though. It was a strange scene: everyone was staring at two people staring at each other to see who would be the first to wink. All the gamblers at the other tables had stopped their betting to become keen spectators. It was as if that contest between the young man and the mysterious, attractive woman was the most important game in the house.

Another minute had passed and it remained a stalemate. It did not look like either one of them would concede any ground; there were no obvious signs of distress on either of their brows. The onlookers in the gambling den were equally anxious. Some were concerned about their bets; others just wanted to know who would have the misfortune of losing an appendage (or maybe even more) that night. It was the highlight of an otherwise routine evening at the gaming house. While all eyes were on the two, no one paid any attention to a new entrant into the room. As if invisible, she moved about undetected amongst all present. Strangely, the Prince, despite the more pressing matter at hand, could see her. He detected movement in the corner of his eyes; in the background where he was not focusing his eyes on, the Prince knew that there was a figure in bright pink moving about very slowly and deliberately. He noticed the almost ghostly apparition some three minutes into the staring contest. Yet, he could not divert his full attention from the young man's eyes. Unable to determine its significance, he paid little heed at first. However, the distance between him and the blurry pink image started to get smaller and smaller as time went by. No one was moving to make way for it; apparently, only the Prince could see it. All of a sudden, well into the eighth minute of the Pinky Winky game, a face darted right in front of the Prince. For a brief moment, the Prince was looking at a face right smack in front of him and it was a spitting image of himself that night. And it blinked! Caught off-guard (plus the Prince thought that the young man seated right across him had given up), the Prince himself blinked as well. It was a mixture of confusion, relief and shock that forced the Prince to give the game away.

Amid the deafening roar of the gamblers surprised by the unexpected result, the dwarf had gotten one of his workers to place a knife with a three-inch blade and a wooden chopping board on the table. The Prince was dumbfounded – where was that woman in bright pink? It was impossible that no one except him had seen her, he thought. Right there and then, the door of the gambling den opened and the Prince looked on in bewilderment as the very woman in bright pink who had just a few moments ago landed him in his current predicament walked into the tense venue. Everyone stepped aside to make way for her as she cut a straight path towards the table where the Prince and the young man were. When she reached the table, she stopped and placed both her hands on the table and leaned slightly forward to look at the Prince and said:

'You don't have to cut off your finger. I will buy over this tavern and waive off your obligation. All you need to do is to bring this young man back home with you. I will follow the both of you.'

Then, the woman in pink straightened herself and looked up to her left where the levitating dwarf was perched in mid-air and addressed him:

'I will give you enough money to last you two lifetimes from operating this den. Deal?'

The dwarf winked at her and called out to his worker to count the money that the woman will soon give to him.

'I will be waiting out at the back. Once it's ready, I will be gone. Whatever happens in this place from now on will be none of my business.' With that, the dwarf whistled happily as he flew off towards the exit at the back of the den.

Like the Prince, the entire house was in shock, albeit for different reasons. The Prince could care less about the ownership of the gambling den. He was still flabbergasted as to why no one could see the woman earlier. Why did she have to walk through the door if she was in the room before? The onlooking crowd was both disappointed and over-whelmed: disappointed because they will not get the sadistic pleasure of witnessing the pain of someone cutting off his pinky; overwhelmed due to the quick transfer of ownership of their favourite joint and the fact that they might never get to see the levitating dwarf who had been a highlight and oddity of many evenings spent there.

The new owner could not be bothered with what the gamblers thought. She was now the owner and she could do anything she wanted. Exercising her new-found authority, she closed the den for the night. To soothe their frustrations at not being able to indulge in their vice, she wrote off everyone's debt up to that night. The hustlers knew a good deal when they were presented with one and they willingly acceded.

In the empty tavern that had just seen an exciting game of Pinky and Winky and a dramatic twist to the game and the fate of the house, the Prince and the young man sat in silence looking at the woman. Without uttering a single word, she headed towards the door. Picking up on the cue, the two men followed her. Under the clear, moonless sky, the woman looked at the Prince and told him to lead them to his home. Knowing that he was in no position to bargain or make any de-mand, he quietly complied. The Prince knew that once he led them to where he stayed, his shameful secret would be exposed. He was fearful for what would happen; at the same time, he knew he was powerless to change his plight. Knowing that this woman had some power un-known to him, he had to comply. Besides, the young man was clearly not on his side; the Prince realised he was alone and he could only be a passive subject in the events to follow that night.

Dread and apprehension were his true companions as the young man and the woman walked closely behind the Prince in the journey to his castle. Upon reaching the foot of his castle tower, the Prince finally addressed his captors:

'I only ask that none of you speak about tonight.'

Expressionless, both of them continued to follow the Prince silently as he led them up the long flight of stairs that brought them to the Prince's room at the very top of the tower.

Once the Prince ushered the two strangers into his room and locked the heavy wooden door, what happened immediately was something that the Prince would not have predicted even in his wildest dream. The woman in pink grabbed the young man and kissed him passionately while she stood inches away from the door. The Prince was obviously taken aback and stepped away. His first instinct was to look away. But he soon realised that he was in the privacy and seclusion of his own dwelling and no one was judging him, least of all the two wanton beings right before him. The young man was not resisting at all and went along with the woman. It was clear to the Prince that the woman was in charge and as he took in the unexpected but stimulating scene before him, the woman seemed to have grown a few inches taller and appeared to physically dominate the ordinary looking young man.

The uncalled-for act of intimacy went on for a few minutes. To the Prince, they looked just like a pair of young lovers who have not seen each other for weeks and were eager to rekindle their desires. It ended abruptly, with the woman disengaging her mouth from her partner's in an indifferent manner, like how one would stop eating because there was something more important to attend to. She stared calmly at the Prince and dictated:

'Now, do what I just did with this boy here. This is what you owe me from earlier.'

The Prince hesitated for a moment. He was after all still royalty. Why should he do what this unknown person was telling him and in his own castle no less? If he resisted, his deepest secret will be apparent. Besides, there were two of them. He had no time to concoct a strategy to counter her. The Prince felt like he had not left the gambling den; he was the loser at the poker table who had run out of cards to play. Even if he tried to bluff, the two strangers had no reason to go along with it. They knew what they were there for and they will not relent until they get it.

As the Prince slowly walked towards the young man, he cannot decide if he will enjoy what was going to happen. Strangely, he felt a slight sense of anticipation and delight building up within him. He knew that the strangers in his room were watching him intently. Yet, this realisation that made him even more self-conscious was causing him to want to commit the act even more. He was going to be in an intimate performance that would liberate him not just from his debt but also from himself. Perhaps, in front of these two seemingly hostile strangers, he could reveal his true self. Since he was not in control and totally unaware of what will take place next, he surrendered to the woman's demand. Feeling unfettered, he stood right in front of the young man, reached out for the back of his neck with his right hand and closed his eyes.

It was something that the Prince had never felt until that point in his life. Finally, he connected with someone. All his life, the Prince never knew where he came from and who his parents were. He had no blood relatives to speak of. Without any background and identity, he imagined himself to be whoever he wanted to be every night once he mastered the magic of changing his outer form. Indulging in physical metamorphosis became the Prince's outlet to solve his existential crisis. The moment he locked lips with the young man from the gambling den, he experienced a wholeness that had eluded him until now. In his mind, he watched a winged-creature descend from the roof of a dark cave. It lowered itself to the cave floor that was sparsely dotted with stalagmites. The Prince could not fully make out the features of the animal as it was dark. It had a long and strong jaw like a gharial and large, round bulging eyes common to tarsiers. Its nose was bulbous with flared nostrils and on top of its head was a white-coloured horn that was about five inches long. Its fully extended wings were jagged like a bat's. The creature's body and lower limbs could not be seen as there was no more light when the Prince tried to look up to the roof of the cave. As the creature neared the ground, it opened its angular jaw. From its mouth, a slimy, orangey tongue revealed itself and slowly, the tiny legs of a baby could be seen. The Prince realised intuitively that he was witnessing his own birth many years ago in the cave that he was conceived in. The truth of his birth lay in being the unnatural offspring of a bat-like creature; he was pushed out of the gastrointestinal tract of a cryptozoological animal. He should be disgusted to learn that he was the vomit of an unknown and monstrous creature. Instead, his heart was filled with joy and euphoria at that epiphanic moment. An important puzzle in his life was solved.

While the Prince was discovering his origin, the young man was also undergoing his own moment of truth. Unknown to the Prince all along, the young man was none other than the accomplice of the woman of hitherto unknown origin. Layla and the gypsy were in cahoots all along. Under her command, the gypsy assumed the form of the young man and Layla projected her image into the Prince's mind during the game of Pinky Winky to first divert his attention and later to confuse him. Now that her plan was working, she was looking forward to relish the moment when she will exact her revenge on the Prince for the severe injustice suffered at his hands (and that of others) in another lifetime and in another form. But her well-laid plan would be thwarted. She was oblivious to an important fact that no one, the gypsy and the Prince included, was privy to before that moment. The intimate physical contact with the Prince sparked off in the young man a deep, rising feeling of fulfilment. He did not know where this emotion come from and he had never before felt that way. His aimless existence thus far meant that the gypsy led an empty and pointless life. At this pivotal point, the gypsy felt that his life was complete; he was finally reunited with his platonic, physical half. Now that the gypsy was whole again and the Prince found reunion with his spiritual half, the myth of Aristophanes was fulfilled. Right in front of Layla, the Prince and the gypsy melded into a single being with four arms and four legs; they were joined at the back of their heads and like the androgynous beings in Aristophanes' myth, they could move only in the same direction if they cartwheeled to where they wanted to go. Now that the spiritual and physical union of the Prince and his long-lost soul was completed, the monstrosity cartwheeled towards Layla who unfortunately had positioned herself near the window of the Prince's room at the top of the tower. Taken aback at the sudden and unimaginable turn of events, Layla took several step backwards as the androgynous form hurtled towards her. In her haste to get as far away from it as quickly as she could, Layla tripped and fell out of the window. Victory was just within her grasp a few moments ago; as she saw the window becoming smaller and smaller as she fell farther and farther away, she rued how she had planned for this her entire life and it would all culminate in an ending that she had not predicted despite her seemingly potent abilities."

The Moon Rabbit

"Just before Layla slammed onto the ground at the foot of the castle tower, just as she had given up all hope, Layla felt that she was being pulled away forcibly sideways and then upwards from her deathbed. Disoriented and confused, all she saw were scenes of white and green alternating before her eyes; white for the clouds in the early morning sky and green for the grass on the ground below. Strangely though, Layla had never felt more secure. Wrapped around her tightly was the sinewy trunk of an ancient and noble creature indebted to Layla.

Layla finally realised what was going on when the whiskered dragon placed her on top of its creased head in between its horns. As it unfurled and unwound its rear section that had just moments ago saved Layla from a certain death, it became apparent to her that the dragon that it had saved several nights ago in the night sky above the ship with Chibuzo on board reappeared out of nowhere to whisk Layla away from her doom. The snow rabbit had been keeping watch over Layla ever since she taught it to hide on the moon. On Earth, the moon and its lone inhabitant could not be seen in the day. But it was not so the other way. Despite turning into a rabbit, the dragon kept its fiery eyes: it could see Layla even during night time on Earth as its eyes illuminated all that they set upon. Seeing Layla's dire predicament, the mythical creature mastered all the magical powers of the moon to appear in the nick of time at the precise moment just before Layla landed. This gargantuan effort cracked the moon's crust, forming the moon craters visible till today. Knowing that it had repaid its debt, the dragon calmly placed Layla near an icy lake on the moon and reverted to its more docile, mammalian form.

Layla and the snow rabbit had only each other as companions on the moon's desolate landscape. Surrounded by a mix of desert and frosted water bodies, it was cold all the time. To keep Layla warm, the rabbit forced itself to grow fur at a rapid rate, shedding them just in time for another new batch to grow. To help Layla stitch the newly shed fur into a jacket, the rabbit spat out saliva that was gooey and when dried, the fur could be made into a thick jacket with several layers for her to stay warm all the time. They constantly stayed with each other and the rabbit would curl itself into a ball next to Layla's stomach whenever they slept. There was plenty of time to sleep on the moon since there was nothing much else to do. In her sleep, Layla did not dream her dreams. Instead, by being in such close physical contact with the ancient, mythical creature, the dragon's past lives were relived by Layla in her countless sleeps on the moon:

In its first life, the dragon was no bigger than a baby green tree snake. But it lived on a planet no bigger than a large watermelon. This made the dragon, albeit small by Earth's standards, the dominant being on that planet. In a week of its existence, it ate up everything on that tiny planet; the insects and animals there were the size of watermelon seeds. Without a food source, the dragon started to gnaw at the crust of the tiny planet, threatening to eat it from inside out. Seeing that, its creator grabbed the dragon and took it out of that small planet and placed it on a bigger planet the size of a hot air balloon. The invisible, nameless creator thought it wise not to make the dragon any bigger than it was. It was a prudent move as the lone snake now had plenty of food. Its prey had time to multiply many-fold at a rate faster than the dragon's appetite. It never ran out of food and it was happy as it was always well-fed. Years went by and the tiny dragon became bored. Listless, it stopped foraging for food as actively as before. It did not comprehend the reason for its existence. Eating was all there was to life, it thought. Nothing else mattered. Eventually, it stopped moving completely. It started to wither from starvation. Seeing its creation degenerate, the formless creator once again took action. It placed another dragon on this second planet, one of a different gender. With a mate, the first dragon sprang to life and procreated. Soon, the planet that was the size of a hot air balloon was bursting with new baby dragons. Food soon ran out and the dragons degenerated into cannibalism. Seeing the sad state of affairs, the creator intervened and threw the remaining surviving dragons onto Earth.

When the dragons that were the size of small tree snakes entered Earth, they flew around the sky. Their smallness in relation to the Earth's size meant that they could float about in the atmosphere effortlessly. They glided about and dominated the skies. Even the birds of prey at the top of the food chain – the eagles, the falcons, the harriers and the like, were no match for the dragons as the new introduction to Earth's skies hunted in groups. They tore the raptors apart and drastically reduced their population. The dragons ruled the skies because of their numbers and their voracious appetite.

The creator took pity on the birds of Earth. It made a pact with the dragons: they will no longer feel hunger and hence they will no longer need to eat. However, the dragons protested. They loved the taste of live flesh and desired to hunt and feed. Doing so provided them with immense satisfaction. The creator dangled a carrot in front of them: in exchange for their need to feed, they would be given the ability to breathe fire. They could use this fire-breathing ability to inflict pain on other living things but they cannot eat anything. The dragons rejoiced. But they wanted more. So, the creator agreed to increase each dragon's physical size by several thousand times to make them look more majestic and powerful. However, if they accepted this, they could no longer breed and procreate. This time, they were elated. The dragons agreed to the creator's conditions. Just like that, the dragons stopped eating and became enormous creatures that breathed fire and dominated the skies. They terrorised animals and later, people (when they started to appear on the planet), even though they no longer had to fear being eaten by the dragons. Every once in a while, non-dragons would be harmed due to the sadistic and narcissistic nature of the dragons to exact pain on others and to feel mighty. Otherwise, the threat of extinction to the other species on Earth due to the dragons' insatiable hunger was eradicated.

On the ship journey to Keltulop, Layla was fascinated and awed by the dragons' majestic form and aura. She thought that they were divine creatures worthy of worship. That was the reason for her grief and empathy when she saw them being massacred in the skies that night with Chibuzo. Layla witnessed the genocidal episode of the dragons' extinction on Earth and she could neither comprehend nor accept the tragic fate of such magnificent creatures. Now, after seeing the dragons' history in her dreams on the moon, she grasped that their violent ending on Earth was entirely their fault; the dragons were hunted out of existence because the people on Earth could no longer put up with their nasty behaviour. The time of the dragons was over and men took over. But thanks to Layla's intervention, one last dragon in the universe remained.

After this revelation, the nights with the moon rabbit were tainted with the knowledge that this innocent looking, harmless bunny was part of a group that had previously inflicted pain and fear on the people back on Earth. The rabbit, however vulnerable it looked now, was complicit in the murder and torture of countless beings back home. Layla almost regretted saving this last creature that she presently hugged to sleep every night. She had not forgotten her life's purpose which could no longer be completed now that she had failed in her plan to get rid of the Prince. And the reason for that plan was because of Layla's previous incarnation who invoked the deadly curse of Jiong to avenge the murder of her parents by bandits in her last life. Without a choice, Layla had to spend her time on the moon, far from her place of vengeance, with a creature who took part in mass murder. It went against every fibre in her being not to squeeze to death the animal nestling in her arms. Yet, Layla was painfully cognisant that doing so would make her no different from the dragons that she had now learnt to unlove. There was no moral difference between killing one and killing many. And Layla's thoughts and actions are far from immaculate: all her life, she had the desire and plan to inflict punishment on someone who had wronged her in her last life. Layla was no innocent.

Every single night since that discovery had been uneasy at best. Layla refrained from showing the moon rabbit too much of her mixed feelings towards it. After all, they were each other's only companion on that unhospitable rock whose purpose was to illuminate half of Earth. Like those on Earth who saw the moon only half the time, Layla had to choose which half of the rabbit-dragon to focus on – the one that saved her or the one that harmed others for its own pleasure. She would spend many sleepless nights resolving this conflict while the creature that elicit both her admiration and hatred was quietly and peacefully enjoying the warmth provided by her body for survival and rest.

It would take eight lunar cycles before Layla made up her mind. The date of her final decision coincided with the eighth full moon of the annual lunar cycle. The dragon rescued her exactly on the last lunar month of the previous year. Just before the moon showed her full, voluptuous sphere for the eighth time that year, Layla held the rabbit in the palm of her hands and announced:

'I am grateful that you saved my life eight months ago. Previously, I have led you to safety here. We do not owe each other anything. We are both alike and distinct in our nature. You have killed many for the sake of doing so; I want to kill for a reason. That does not make me different, I know, from you. Killing is what it is regardless of the rationale behind the act. I cannot reconcile this but I have to do it, still. Grant me your help in my quest for vengeance and I promise you that I will stay here with you forever to provide warmth and shelter for you.'

Layla brought her head forward slightly and whispered into the rabbit's long ears. Even though there was no one else on that tiny star in a vast galaxy in an even bigger universe, she cannot risk having the possibility that her plan might fail again just because she was too callous in relaying it to the rabbit. When Layla was done, she lifted the rabbit with both her hands high above her head. With much effort, the rabbit leapt into the air before Layla and flew towards the sky above her. As it did so, the rotund shape of the moon rabbit thinned and elongated into a serpentine form: it was transforming itself into its original form for its journey back to Earth.

Once it entered the sky on Earth, the last dragon quickly turned into a piece of goose feather and delicately descended to the ground below. It seemed purposeless, letting the winds decide which way it would fall. Yet, the dragon had a course of action, one that had already been chartered by Layla who was watching it closely from the moon.

The feather ended its flight on the wooden doorstep of a farmer and his wife whose humble hut and family farm plot lay next to a tributary of the Yellow River. Once on the wooden steps of the hut, the feather became a naked, wailing baby. Startled by the unexpected cries of an infant while having their simple mid-day meal of congee with salted cabbage, the childless couple hurriedly opened the front door of their home to trace the source of the cries. Shocked at their startling discovery, they quickly picked up the baby girl and wrapped her with a long, cotton cloth that the woman used as skirt.

In the days and months that followed, the couple committed to sacrificing themselves for the girl. Childless and past her fertile years, the woman had only just lamented to her husband their barren fate the night before heaven blessed them with the surprise package at their doorstep. They decided to name her 'Voice from the Heart' because to the couple, that was where she came from – their hearts. Without a source of milk, the couple sold off half of their farm plot to raise money to pay for a wet nurse. They were also lucky to have good weather during the years that Voice from the Heart was growing up. With bumper harvests year after year, they had little difficulty to pay for the girl's food and clothing and they even managed to save enough money to repurchase the farm plot that they had earlier sold off. Grateful for their good fortune, the couple never forgot to honour the deities and their ancestors.

When she turned eight, Voice from the Heart started formal schooling. In the first few years, she walked two miles to a village school that had only forty students. It would be an uneventful few years. Nothing special or untoward would take place in this village school. The time would come when Voice from the Heart would grow older and continue her education in a larger school for older children. She would have to travel by boat along the tributary to reach the school as it would take half a day to traverse the 30 miles of cultivated padi fields and small hills to reach it by foot. The boat journey would use up only three hours by comparison. So, every Sunday evening, she would report to the school's hostel and stay there until late Friday afternoon when she would make her way back home to see her adopted parents. The school was attended by children like Voice from the Heart who lived in the counties and villages in a 50-mile radius. And most of them would have similar living and travelling arrangements as Voice from the Heart.

The events that Layla had planned for would unfurl in ways that she never would have imagined when she released the rabbit from her palms on the moon several years ago. The turning point came in the fourth and last year of Voice from the Heart's time in this school. At the start of her fourth school year, she would have a new classmate; this new addition was completely new to the school. When this fresh arrival first entered the school's compound, everyone was curious – she had dark, chocolate brown complexion unlike the light yellow skin tone that was common to people in those parts. She could not speak the local language but strangely, she could write using their script. It was because of her ability to write (and she could write very well in the local language) that the school decided to accept her and teach her how to verbalise the symbols used by the language. She could not even tell them her name at first and because her favourite activity during playtime was to gather tiny bamboo shoots and stick them to the mud on the ground to form various patterns, they called her Bamboo Pillar. This nickname would stick with her throughout her time at the school.

Unlike the other children who went home on Fridays, Bamboo Pillar lived in the school hostel all the time. Once, Voice from the Heart's parents fell violently ill with a contagious cold that lasted a month. Afraid that they might pass the illness to their beloved adopted daughter, her parents sent a written note to the school to explain their situation and asked that Voice from the Heart be allowed to remain in school for the next few weekends. Their request was granted. In those long weekends that followed, Voice from the Heart was left alone with Bamboo Pillar in the school. The only other person in the school with them was a female worker who cooked and cleaned for them as everyone, including the principal, would have returned home. This worker left them alone to their own devices. It was during this period that Voice from the Heart and Bamboo Pillar became closer and their intimacy would unhinge Layla's plan.

Voice from the Heart was a naïve and innocent girl who had never known much else besides her parents' love and what she was taught at school. Bamboo Pillar fascinated her because this new arrival to her life was full of tricks. This was a side of Bamboo Pillar that Voice from the Heart had not seen until she had to spend those weekends away

     CHASING CINDERELLA — BROKEN DREAMS BY A.C.K. MIN

from home. During school time, when everyone was around, Bamboo Pillar merely arranged bamboo shoots in ways that seemed to make no sense. It looked random and haphazard to everyone. The first day that they spent alone together, Bamboo Pillar placed ten bamboo shoots in a remote part of the school compound. She told Voice from the Heart to close her eyes for five seconds. When Voice from the Heart looked at the bamboo shoots five seconds later, they had turned into full grown bamboo plants that were three-foot tall. Bamboo Pillar would show Voice from the Heart many other tricks in the weekends that they spent together. She would make the bamboo plants disappear and flower at will. Voice from the Heart was captivated as she knew that it was very rare for bamboo plants to flower. Her parents told her that one could live an entire cycle of the zodiac and never get to see flowers grow on a bamboo plant. Voice from the Heart cannot wait to go home and tell her parents what she had seen in the weeks that she had spent with Bamboo Pillar.

The girls quickly became the best of friends. Bamboo Pillar showed Voice from the Heart a world of magic that was previously unknown to her. In turn, Voice from the Heart taught Bamboo Pillar how to master the accent of the local language as Bamboo Pillar tend to mispronounce words due to the tonal nature of the language. Voice from the Heart looked forward to every Friday in that month when her parents were sick as she knew she would have more time to spend alone with Bamboo Pillar. By the second Saturday of that month, the girls were already sleeping on the same bed at night. They were like inseparable twin sisters.

In the third weekend of that month, Voice from the Heart and Bamboo Pillar hugged each other to sleep like they did the past weekend (when the other children were sleeping in the shared hostel rooms on weekdays, the two girls would sleep separately in their own beds). That Friday night, Voice from the Heart could feel many hands touching her body from head to toe. They were light, gentle strokes and Voice from the Heart found comfort in these touches. In her sleep, she dreamt that her parents were stroking her lightly when she was still an infant. She felt secure and loved that night and continued to sleep soundly. The next night, Voice from the Heart experienced the same. The only difference was that she could sense that the touches became slightly stronger and more eager unlike the night before. Still, she was happy with the caresses and slept soundly throughout the night. The next night, it became unusual and unexpected as Voice from the Heart knew she was sleeping alone as the other children had returned to the school on Sunday night to prepare for the school week ahead. That night, she felt many hands groping her from top to bottom and she opened her eyes to find out what was going on since Bamboo Pillar was not supposed to be sleeping on the same bed with her. Tried as she might, Voice from the Heart could not see anything. She felt something, a hand most likely, covering her eyes and preventing her from finding out what was happening and who was responsible for it. Confused and fearful, she tried to scream but an even stronger force pressed her lips together. Voice from the Heart could hardly let out a whimper throughout the ordeal that lasted till dawn.

In the morning, Voice from the Heart woke up frazzled and confused. She confided in Bamboo Pillar during the first break of the school day. Bamboo Pillar listened patiently to and her and offered her comfort, telling her she would watch over her that night. Voice from the Heart cheered up knowing that someone would look out for her. Even though she was still haunted by the events of the previous night, Voice from the Heart crept into bed that night and shut her eyes. Just before she did so, she glanced at Bamboo Pillar who was in the bed diagonally opposite her to the right. She saw Bamboo Pillar's big, round eyes and Voice from the Heart let out a slight smile before she tried to sleep. It took a longer time for her to fall asleep that night as she was still apprehensive and nervous. Slowly but surely, she fell into a deep slumber and woke up only in the morning when everyone around her in the room were busy tottering about getting ready for school. Nothing happened the previous night and Voice from the Heart felt refreshed and just a little safer. Fortunately for her, the rest of the nights that week would pass by uneventfully. Voice from the Heart was glad that the torment of that unbearable night did not revisit her.

On the fourth and last Sunday that Voice from the Heart would spend alone with Bamboo Pillar in the school, Bamboo Pillar planted several bamboo shoots in a circular fashion on a patch of grass near the back gate of the school. She invited Voice from the Heart to the centre of the circle within the bamboo shoots. In front of Voice from the Heart, Bamboo Pillar raised her arms upwards and the bamboo shoots that were only a few inches tall quickly grew to six-feet high. Of course, Voice from the Heart already knew about Bamboo Pillar's ability, having seen many other tricks she had performed in front of her over the many weekends they have spent with each other. So now, the two girls were surrounded by a wall of bamboo plants taller than them, effectively blocking off any prying eyes from the outside. Smiling, Bamboo Pillar walked towards Voice from the Heart and asked her to close her eyes. Expecting a new magic trick, Voice from the Heart unquestioningly did as she was asked. When she opened her eyes, Voice from the Heart saw before her a large ball-like shape with four legs and four arms. It looked comical to her as it reminded her of a lump of dough with many limbs. She laughed and was glad that her best friend had thought of a new way to amuse her. The ball rolled towards her by performing a few cartwheels with its limbs. Stopping just in front of Voice from the Heart, Bamboo Pillar's latest magical manifestation circled her and started to lay its many limbs on her. Alternating between using its hands and feet, the elliptical phenomenon was stunning in its attention to detail; it left no spot on its victim's body untouched. By now, Voice from the Heart knew that the creature encircling and molesting her was the tormentor from that night and not a friend of hers. She opened her mouth to let out a horrifying scream; she was reliving her nightmare in broad daylight. It was a dreadful reminder that what happened several nights ago was not a figment of her imagination. Her effort to call for help and release her pent-up fears ended in failure as the abominable creature stuffed one of its arms into her gaping mouth and down her throat. As she gagged and threw up, the androgynous creation invaded Voice from the Heart via other orifices – her vagina, anus, ears and nostrils, using its fingers for the smaller openings. It even found time to take out an arm (or finger) and reinserted it into other holes. Voice from the Heart was completely helpless and at the mercy of her oppressor. Weakened and in severe pain from being forcibly penetrated in the most intimate and private areas, she had long given up. The battle was effectively over the moment she placed complete trust in Bamboo Pillar.

The ordeal must have gone on for a few hours because the next thing that Voice from the Heart remembered was waking up to see the setting sun – it was just about noon when Bamboo Pillar invited her to the centre of the encirclement created by the bamboo palisade. She remembered the position of the sun high up in the sky because that was the only thing she looked at in desperation as Bamboo Pillar jammed its limbs into her, stopping her from articulating any protest at being violated and raped in every and any possible way. Her pupils dilated as she searched for meaning in the heavens for her suffering on Earth. She had hoped that night would come soon and the fastest way to see darkness would be to let the sun's relentless rays blind her eyes. All she wanted then was to remove all her senses so that she would not feel or see and hence there would be no suffering. Her wish was almost granted as she opened her eyes to witness a crimson sky as day made way for night. Voice from the Heart cannot wait to see the moon reappear and then she can beg Layla to let her return to her safe abode far away from this present state of grief.

But her wish would not be granted. That night, the moon was not to be seen. Unusually cloudy, not a sliver of light from the guardian of the night reached the ground where she lay. She wished that she was not under Layla's control. If not, she would have instantly transformed into the terrifying dragon that she really was and torch the place to the ground. She had a mission and she would stick to the letter of Layla's instructions. She would wait patiently to return home at the end of the school week and bide her time. When the school week restarted the next day, Bamboo Pillar was nowhere to be found. The school conducted an unsuccessful search for her on its grounds. Strangely, when the principal and head teachers checked her records, they discovered to their annoyance that they did not have the details and particulars of Bamboo Pillar's family and residence. For some reason unknown to everyone, Bamboo Pillar allowed herself to be admitted into the school without filling out the necessary documentation. While the rest of the school was flabbergasted, Voice from the Heart was glad that she did not have to face the cause of her emotional and physical distress anymore."

FUTILITY

Ngurunguur looked at the cast of eternity before him. He was confident that he had done justice to his storytelling; so far, he had managed to cull disparate threads and characters from different narrators and tales into a coherent storyline of his own. No one had challenged him since he took control from the salt merchant. The tale of Layla and the moon rabbit would come to a conclusion that would be decided by Ngurunguur. Without seeking approval from anyone, he continued:

"Reaching the comfort of her own home after a month spent living in the school hostel, Voice from the Heart fell into a deep sleep. She would not wake for two weeks. During that time, her adopted parents were at their wits' end. They simply did not know why their adopted child, who had been healthy and had given them nothing but joy in her short life, had fallen to such a woeful state. She did not show any sign of fever and would not respond to any attempt to wake her. Voice from the Heart would not even open her lips to take water or food. In their desperation, the aging couple sought the help of anyone they could think of – the village doctors, priests and even witch doctors. The remedies offered ranged from the sane to the ludicrous. Doctors advised the couple to make a mash of vegetables and gently insert it into the patient's mouth. Priests from the village temple wrote talismans using an ancient script and pasted them on her forehead. Witch doctors would burn chickens alive and grind their bones into fine ash powder and sprinkle them all over Voice from the Heart's body and bed. None of these methods worked. She remained stubborn in her quest for tranquillity and solace.

Exactly fourteen days since she fell into her comatose state, Voice from the Heart woke up and her parents, elated that their precious gem had risen from her vegetative state, hugged her and cried. They did not know if they were crying because they were relieved, happy or simply giving vent to the innumerable minutes and seconds that they had spent worrying over her. Regardless, they were thankful that their daughter, whom they have treated and regarded as their own since the day they found her at their doorstep, was alive and well. She showed no symptom of illness or demonic possession (as the priests and witch doctors would have her parents believe) and looked and behaved every bit her usual self. Slowly, as the days passed, her parents were convinced that their daughter was fine and life could go on as before.

To the dragon, there was nothing wrong. It merely wanted to rest and more importantly to have time to resolve a conflict that was gnawing within her: she wanted to escape from Layla, not follow her secret plan and not have to return to the moon to live for eternity. The dragon knew that this betrayal would mean that she risked roaming Earth in human form forever. And that would mean that her once magnificent species will come to its final, irreversible end. It was a risk the dragon was willing to take as it did not want to return to the moon and be subjected indefinitely to Layla's whims and fancies. For this plan to work, the dragon must first stay out of sight of the moon's prying eye. Lying in bed in her parents' hut for two weeks was the beginning of the dragon's selfish plot.

However, the dragon did not manage to concoct a fool proof plan in the two weeks that she appeared sick and removed from the world around her. Running away under the cover of darkness at night was not an option as the moon would illuminate Voice from the Heart's movements for Layla. In the day, everyone in her village would see what she was doing. Turning into a dragon was of course a sure-fire way to fail. Voice from the Heart decided to wake up and observe the opportunities around her. At least she might be able to take advantage of any chance to escape if they presented themselves at the right moment. Lying inert was too passive an approach for Voice from the Heart to improve her situation.

It would resolve not to step out in the open, be it night or day, so that Layla would not get to monitor her movement. To do that, Voice from the Heart convinced her parents that she would no longer go to school. It was easy as they would agree to any first request from their daughter whom they thought had just returned to them from the brink of death. The excuse that she gave was that she was tired and breathless. She did not even want to leave the hut to tend to the fields or to take a stroll. Her parents acceded without question; they were simply glad that Voice from the Heart was no longer unresponsive and bedridden.

Her decision not to venture an inch outside was fortuitously supported by news that a band of men had been pillaging nearby villages with extreme violence. They would strike when everyone was asleep, breaking down doors with sheer brute force and then shouting at the top of their voices, clanging their metal weapons – machetes, poles, axes…, to intimidate and scare their victims. Numbering over ten men each time, the midnight burglars struck fear and trepidation in the region. Afraid for their daughter's safety, Voice from the Heart's parents thought that it was best that she did not travel to school anyway and if she wanted to stay indoors all the time, then so be it. After a three-week frenzy of news of violent crime in the surrounding areas, the spate of attacks by the unknown bandits died down. For two weeks after the last attack which saw a family of five, whose father was a blacksmith, burnt alive after being impaled separately on poles driven to the ground, there was no more report of violence or break-ins. Gradually and cautiously, everyone became more relaxed and felt safer. Slowly, life returned to normal.

What the villagers did not know was that the attacks tapered off not because the bandits left for elsewhere. The marauding band of criminals were decimated by something much more menacing than them. While they were resting in the day time in a secluded grotto, a tiny ball rolled into their cave. It stopped the moment it was seen by the first man (altogether, there were about thirty of them). Seconds later, it started rolling, changing direction in no recognisable pattern on the floor of the cave. By then, all the men had either risen to their feet or sat up to watch the strange phenomenon in the cave. Assured of everyone's attention, the ball rose to mid-air and unexpectedly enlarged by several times. At the same time, it flattened out so that it took on an oblong form than remain in its original shape of a perfectly shaped sphere. To everyone's horror and astonishment, the bizarre entity grew limbs – four arms and four legs to be exact. Before the hardened outlaws could recover from their shock, the creature spun violently towards one of them, killing him instantly. It continued hurtling towards its targets randomly and even bounced off the walls, roof and floor of the cave, sometimes rolling on the floor, sometimes flying in mid-air, decimating anyone who got in the way of its wanton, senseless destruction. When all the strong men lay dead on the cave floor, the creature rolled around and gathered the bodies to the center of the grotto. Then, it started to consume their flesh and bones for the next five days, stopping only to take small breaks in between. It made sure that nothing – not even hair or blood, was wasted in its feeding frenzy.

After its many-day meal of villains, the creature decided to rest for the next sixteen days. When it woke up from its break, the creature had acquired new powers from eating the flesh and souls of so many men. It had the ability to transfigure and multiply itself into anything it wanted to and however many it wished. Grinning, it stepped out of the grotto into the open and welcomed the feel of the morning sun on its faces. It looked out into the horizon and fantasised about the multiple sufferings it would inflict using its new-found powers.

The day that the creature ventured out of the grotto was also the day that Voice from the Heart's parents decided to go to the town centre at night. It was after all the fifteenth day of the eighth lunar month of the year and it was customary for families all over the country to commemorate the auspicious date that symbolised family togetherness. The moon, said to be especially round that time of the year, reflected the harmony and joy of family ties. Knowing that their daughter would not make an exception even for that night, Voice from the Heart's parents left a mooncake baked with lotus paste and seeds for her to eat after their family dinner before leaving for the town centre to take part in the festivities. Unfortunately for Voice from the Heart, while her parents took in the numerous sights and watched the plentiful performances on the streets in the center of town, the young girl would meet her tragic and violent end.

Turning and multiplying itself into five rough men brandishing axes, the creature revived the havoc that the villages along the Yellow River tributaries had not seen for two weeks. That night, entire families were hacked to death at their dinner tables while eating their festival reunion meal. The bandits even stayed after each massacre to help themselves to the food left behind by the people they had just slaughtered. Amidst the blood and chopped up body parts, the amoral beasts laughed and joked as if they were enjoying a feast in their own home. Their appetite for food seemed unable to be satiated as they continued to gorge house after house; only their tendency to get drunk made them somewhat identical with their human victims. After decimating some ten families, the soulless men decided to call a stop to the night's carnage and made their way back to the grotto.

In their inebriated state, they somehow lost their bearings. Instead of travelling inland away from the river and its tributaries, the drunk men followed the water, stumbling and rolling along the way, at times almost falling into it. It was almost two hours before the first light of dawn greeted the new day that one of them finally realised that they had been heading the wrong way all that time. Looking towards the hills (the full moon helped to show the way in the clear night sky), they headed towards the general direction of their secret hideout. It was fate that they stumbled over a low wooden fence protecting some small rice fields. Undeterred, they climbed over the fencing and found the doorsteps of a wooden hut. Laughing at their good fortune, they decided to spring a surprise on the hut's occupants by entering it as quietly as possible. The men found it hilarious that for the first time in their night of debauchery and bloodshed, they were creeping surreptitiously into a house to eventually wreck mindless mayhem.

The men found Voice from the Heart fast asleep in her bed. Keeping with their impromptu plan of executing their devious deeds silently, four of them covered the victim's eyes, mouth, nose and held her limbs down to prevent her from shouting and struggling. The fifth man positioned himself between her thighs and proceeded to violate her after tearing away her night clothes. Faced with the might and brutality of five ruffians, Voice from the Heart was powerless to put up any resistance. She gagged and writhed as the men abused her one after another, over and over. They stopped only when her parents finally arrived home after a night's trek back from the town. Once the scumbags realised that their revelry was interrupted by the return of the couple, one of them smashed the head of Voice from the Heart with the knob of his axe, rendering her unconscious. The men then proceeded to cut her parents down with their weapons and returned to her almost lifeless body and continued to rape her. When they were finally tired of their repugnant deed, it was almost noon. They chopped up her body into several pieces using their axes before laying down on the floor of the bloodied hut, waking up only after the sun had set. Before they left for the grotto, the men collected the hacked body parts that were strewn all over the hut and wrapped them inside a white cotton cloth that they found in her parents' bedroom: it was the same cloth that her adopted mother had used to wrap Voice from the Heart when she first found her abandoned on the steps of the hut many years ago. It was then callously thrown into an irrigated padi field that belonged to the executed family."

Hell was silent the moment Ngurunguur stopped. They knew about Voice from the Heart's past and Ngurunguur just took extreme liberties with it. The attention of all souls was now directed at Voice from the Heart. She stared angrily at Ngurunguur who completely changed her life story. From living in a swampy area, Ngurunguur had placed her in a riverine locale. Her parents were not murdered; Ngurunguur deemed it fit to have them killed just to make his story more exciting. And to have her raped by the transfigurative offshoots of a mythical creature instead of actual men with souls (however damned they were), she had been violated yet again even after her death centuries earlier.

Furthermore, she was never abused in school by some monster; nor did she stay at home during the night of her death to avoid being seen by the moon. She was really a filial daughter who wanted her parents to enjoy that night's festivities while she remained at home to clean up after their family dinner. Indignant, she wished she had not let the master storyteller gain control of the narrative. But it was too late as the Devil had heard enough to make up his mind.

For his efforts in recreating the tale of the origins of the moon fairy and the rabbit, Ngurunguur would be given the ultimate prize of rebirth by the Devil. The Devil was entertained by how Ngurunguur mangled the life of Voice from the Heart and gave it a bizarre, nasty flavour with Aristophanes' misdemeanours. Most importantly, Ngurunguur managed to stave off the challenges to the trophy from many others by subverting their stories to fit into his own. In any case, the Devil did not care about Voice from the Heart's feelings. It asked for a good story and the Devil had gotten one.

Stuck on the moon and blind to the developments in hell, Layla the moon fairy had no clue how she lost her moon rabbit to Ngurunguur. In her grief and longing, she created a massive imprint of a rabbit's head with two ears on the surface of the moon with her tears to serve as a reminder to the dragon that it must still execute her plan and return to her once it sees the sign in the night sky. Elsewhere, in a desolate and forgotten corner on Earth, the tears of a prince disappeared before they touched the ground where he lay; his reunion with Cinderella was not to be and besides, he still had to wrestle with the depravity of his soul and the hideousness of his physical form.

EPILOGUE

Ngurunguur's rebirth was short-lived. The moment he reappeared as a tiny mouse on earth, his soul was extinguished when a kookaburra devoured it. The Devil honoured its word; it was also a tricky bastard. None of hell's inhabitants knew about this and the Devil had just started to erase the stories of humankind one storyteller at a time.